Fill My Empty Heart

Judy Baer

For Sharon Madison,
who always speaks
with a smile in her voice.

Cedar River Daydreams (for girls 12–15):

1. *New Girl in Town*
2. *Trouble with a Capital "T"*
3. *Jennifer's Secret*
4. *Journey to Nowhere*
5. *Broken Promises*
6. *The Intruder*
7. *Silent Tears No More*
8. *Fill My Empty Heart*
9. *Yesterday's Dream*
10. *Tomorrow's Promise*

Springflower Books (for girls 12–15):

Adrienne   *Melissa*
Erica   *Michelle*
Jill   *Paige*
Laina   *Sara*
Lisa   *Wendy*
Marty

Heartsong Books (for young adults):

Andrea   *Kara*
Anne   *Karen*
Carrie   *Leslie*
Colleen   *Rachel*
Cynthia   *Shelly*
Gillian   *Sherri*
Jenny   *Stacey*
Jocelyn   *Tiffany*

"Don't you know that you yourselves are God's temple and that God's Spirit lives in you? If anyone destroys God's temple, God will destroy him; for God's temple is sacred, and you are that temple."
1 Corinthians 3:16–17

Chapter One

The Hamburger Shack was buzzing with activity. The jukebox, fed an endless string of quarters, was playing at full volume.

Egg McNaughton hunched over a table intently scooping yogurt into his mouth. The bright yellow, string-net muscle shirt he wore only emphasized the scrawniness of his arms and shoulders. Egg put his spoon down to take another bite of the tofu burger heaped with bean sprouts and white cheese, which he had brought from home.

With a look of distaste, Binky McNaughton watched her brother devour the unsavory combination before turning back to her ice cream sundae topped with marshmallow, butterscotch and bananas.

Jennifer Golden was zealously devouring her own sundae, paying no attention to Egg or his sister. Across from her, Todd Winston and Lexi Leighton shared a banana split.

Jennifer was the first to speak. "Have you seen the new student teacher Coach Derek has this quarter?" Her eyes glowed with the thought. She licked her lips and grinned. "What a hunk!"

Mr. Evan Cartwright was big talk around Cedar River High School. There'd always been a trail of student teachers through the school, but this particular one had sparked more interest than the others.

"He's got the most incredibly gorgeous hair." Binky touched her own light reddish-brown hair, and said wistfully, "He looks like a lifeguard from some California beach."

Jennifer nodded dreamily. " 'Sun-kissed hair.' That's what I call it."

For a moment Lexi thought Egg was going to choke on his tofu burger.

" 'Sun-kissed hair!' " he echoed. "What's that supposed to mean?"

"You know. All shades of color. Really blond on top, like the sun has bleached it out," Lexi explained.

"He knows what I mean," Jennifer said confidently. "He's just jealous 'cause *his* hair isn't sunkissed."

Binky studied her brother's hair. "Yeah. Egg's hair looks more like it was kissed by the stump of an old tree—or Matt Windsor's grubby cowboy boots. Or, maybe—"

"Knock it off!" Egg blurted. "And I'm sick of hearing about the student teacher's hair, too."

"Then, let's talk about his eyes," Binky chirped.

Lexi put a hand over her mouth so Egg wouldn't see her grin.

"Have you ever seen eyes that blue before?"

"They're as blue as the sky or the ocean—or both."

"His eyes may be beautiful," Jennifer admitted, "but I think it's his muscles that do it for me."

Egg made gagging sounds over his sandwich.

Jennifer turned to him with a cool, appraising stare. "See? I knew he'd choke on that stuff if he ate enough of it."

"It's not my food that's making me sick. It's this conversation."

"Actually," Todd interjected, "I think Jennifer has a point. I heard Mr. Cartwright was a champion weight lifter."

That statement got Egg's attention. "Really?" Egg had been lifting weights for some time. It was his goal to bulk up and impress Minda Hannaford. So far, he hadn't done any bulking and he certainly hadn't impressed Minda, but he hadn't given up hope.

"He's a football player, too," Todd went on. "One of the guys said he's being watched by the professionals."

"How come a guy like that gets it all?" Egg's voice trailed away as he looked ruefully down at his muscle shirt hanging loosely from his scrawny frame.

Todd chuckled. "Don't give up hope, Egg. He'll be teaching Phy. Ed. and coaching under Coach Derek. Maybe he can give you a few tips on weight lifting."

Egg looked at Todd wistfully. "Do you think so?"

Lexi felt sympathy for her tall, thin friend. Egg would like nothing more than to have a build like Mr. Cartwright's. Instead, his was more like the stick figures her little brother Ben drew with his crayons.

"Don't feel bad, Egg," Todd said with a smile. "You'll have to accept the fact that it's not in your genes to have bulky muscles. You're more of a race-horse kind of guy. A runner. The long, lean, quick body type."

"It's not so important to be all muscles," Lexi interjected. "I don't think Mr. Cartwright looks that great."

Egg sighed again and looked at his food with sudden distaste. He'd been stuffing himself full of yogurt and tofu for weeks. He'd been mixing protein drinks out of vile substances and acting like sugar was a form of arsenic. And for all his trouble, he didn't look any stronger or healthier than Todd, who was polishing off the last of the banana split.

Egg plucked at a bean sprout which had fallen from his sandwich. "Maybe you're right, Todd. I'll bet Mr. Cartwright could give me some tips on bulking up. He probably knows all kinds of things that Coach doesn't."

"Speaking of differences," Jennifer interjected, "have any of you seen Anna Marie Arnold lately?"

Anna Marie was a shy girl, with soft brown curls and a dreamy, unapproachable look. Because of her shyness, she tended to keep people at a distance and was hesitant to smile. Lexi sensed that Anna Marie was self-conscious about her size and weight. She'd often heard Anna called by her nickname "Banana Anna." The name had come from Anna Marie's love of banana splits. But Anna Marie was not the same girl she was the first time Lexi had met her.

"She's lost weight, hasn't she?" Binky asked.

Jennifer nodded. "She's been dieting. Poor girl. I suppose she just couldn't stand it anymore."

"What do you mean?" Lexi wondered. Because she was relatively new in town, she didn't know the history of all the students at Cedar River.

Todd took Lexi's hand. "For a long time, Anna Marie was the butt of a lot of rotten tricks and jokes. A lot of the kids used to call her names."

"Yeah, I remember 'Flap-Flap Thighs,'" Binky pointed out.

"And 'Thunder-Thighs,'" Jennifer added.

"And 'Chubola.'"

"That's horrible," Lexi groaned.

"And that's not the worst of it," Todd interjected.

"Remember the mean tricks they used to play?" Binky piped.

Egg and Jennifer nodded. "Kids would steal her lunch and refuse to tell her where they'd hid it," Jennifer said. "Sometimes Anna Marie would spend the whole noon hour looking around the school yard for her sandwich."

"Why would they do that?" Lexi asked.

"Oh," Egg shrugged, "they'd tell her that she didn't need lunch because she already had one too many lunches stored on her already."

Lexi's lips tightened in a grim line.

"Once a group of girls stole her coat and hat and made a scarecrow out of them on the playground," Binky said indignantly. "They stuffed the coat and hat full of fall leaves so the scarecrow was big and fat, and they said it looked like Anna Marie."

"I think that's the most horrible thing I've ever heard," Lexi protested. "How hateful!"

Jennifer shook her head morosely. "Oh, that isn't the worst. The Phy. Ed. stories are the worst."

Lexi was almost afraid to ask. "What do you mean?"

"I was in Anna Marie's Phy. Ed. class. Our teacher didn't like overweight people. There were two or three in the class, and she would make them run extra laps and do extra jumping jacks because she said they needed to get rid of their fat. Once, she made the three overweight kids run around the gym six extra times. Anna Marie wasn't used to that and she fainted."

"Oh, no! What happened then?"

"The teacher got reprimanded, that's all," Jennifer shrugged.

"It's mean," Binky piped up. "Anna Marie is a nice girl, too. I don't know why people have to be so cruel."

"I don't blame her for starting to diet. After all those years of teasing, she's probably decided she doesn't want it to happen anymore," Jennifer added.

Todd turned to Lexi, swept a wisp of hair away from her cheek and asked gently, "What are you thinking about?"

"I was thinking about how horrible people can be. Being fat or thin doesn't make you the kind of person you are."

"Too true," Binky agreed.

"And isn't it crazy," Lexi went on, "that Egg wants to be bigger and Anna Marie wants to be smaller. Nobody's satisfied with the way they are! God made us all different, all wonderful. I wonder why we can't just appreciate the way we are and enjoy life."

"That's easy for you to say," Binky said. "You're practically perfect. Maybe if you had some flaws, you'd understand how skinny people like us or heavy people like Anna Marie feel."

"Ha!" Lexi protested. "Have you seen how skinny my legs look in a bathing suit? You call that perfect?"

Jennifer gave a snort from her side of the table. "I figure I have just the opposite problem. That nickname Thunder-Thighs? Fits me too."

"I don't feel sorry for either one of you," Binky chimed in. "My mom's still buying clothes for me in the junior-high section. The way I figure it, I'll be buying clothes in the children's department until I'm ninety years old."

Suddenly, Todd clamped his hands over his ears and moaned as if he were in great pain.

"What's wrong?" Binky asked.

"I can't take it anymore. I can't take it anymore," Todd dropped his head to the table and groaned. He lifted his head and stared around at the three girls with glazed eyes. "Don't tell me these things. I always thought all three of you were perfect."

"We'd better keep our mouths shut," Lexi said with a giggle. "Todd will be thinking of all the things we've told him about ourselves, instead of thinking we're perfect."

"I blew it," Binky said with a groan.

Jennifer's eyes twinkled knowingly. "Don't worry. I think Harry Cramer still thinks you're all right, Binky."

The satisfied expression of a kitten who'd just lapped a bowl of cream crossed Binky's face.

"If we've got some bad traits, I guess we should accept them, and if we've got some good traits, we should realize that we can't take credit for them," Lexi said quietly. "God made us. That should be good enough."

"Only you would think of it that way, Lexi," Binky announced. "You're the only person I know that looks at life through Bible-colored lenses."

Bible-colored lenses? Lexi rolled the term around in her mind. She liked it. It was certainly a view that made the world look a lot brighter.

"You guys want anything more?"

Lexi looked up to see Jerry Randle standing at the foot of their table with a pad and pencil in hand. Jerry was looking happier, Lexi noticed. Though he was the first person she'd met when she came to Cedar River, Lexi still didn't feel she knew him very well. Lexi suspected he was lonely. Jerry lived with his aunt and uncle while his parents worked overseas for long periods of time.

"No, thanks," Jennifer said. "I'd better not, otherwise I won't be able to eat supper."

"Me either," Binky agreed. "We're having roast beef and mashed potatoes and gravy for supper."

Egg whimpered. "Really?"

"Of course." Binky added, "Egg will probably get Mom to broil him a couple of chicken breasts or something. I think he's watching his cholesterol."

Jerry laughed out loud. "Egg's watching everything," he said pointedly. "Just so Minda will start to watch him."

Lexi saw a blush of red creep up Egg's neck and spread across his cheeks.

Jerry and Minda were dating. Even though Jerry knew that Egg had a mad crush on his girlfriend, he wasn't intimidated by this improbable competitor for Minda's affection.

"How about you, Lexi?" Todd asked. "Do you want anything else to eat?"

"No, thanks. I promised Ben that we'd put together a puzzle tonight. I'm sure he's sitting at the card table in the living room right now, twiddling his thumbs and wondering where I am."

As Jerry turned away to return to the counter, the bell which signaled a new customer began to jingle. "Hey, Harry, over here!" Todd called and waved Harry Cramer toward their table. Binky lit up like a Christmas tree. Her smile was so bright and sparkly that she virtually beamed.

"I thought I might find you here," Harry said. Harry Cramer, a tall, good-natured, even-tempered young man, had hazel eyes that always danced with good humor. His naturally curly hair and the chip in his front tooth made him seem approachable and friendly. "I was wondering if anyone needed a ride home."

"Anyone other than Binky, you mean?" Jennifer asked bluntly. Harry grinned sheepishly. "Well, if you absolutely must have a ride home, Golden, I'll give you one."

Jennifer turned her nose in the air. "No thanks, Cramer. I wouldn't dream of being somewhere I wasn't wanted."

While the playful bantering was going on, Binky gathered her things together and stood up. "Well, I'd *love* a ride home," she said. She scooted out from behind the table and walked out with Harry.

"Time for us to go, too," Todd murmured. Lexi nodded and tucked her hand into the crook of his arm and they left the Hamburger Shack together.

Chapter Two

"Where are you going, Lexi?" Jennifer wondered as Lexi hurriedly gathered files from her locker. The early morning hum of students changing classes echoed through the school's hallways.

"I have to go to the *River Review* office," Lexi said with a grimace. "I have to type captions for the photos I took for the next edition of the school paper. I should have had them in yesterday."

"Lexi Leighton, late?" Jennifer acted as though the impossible had happened. "How can that be?"

"I had to go to my dad's veterinary clinic last night and catch up on some work. There were about two dozen cages to wash down."

"Yuck," Jennifer wrinkled her nose. "I'm sorry I asked. You'd better get going or you won't get those captions done."

Lexi hurried toward the *River Review* office. She loved being a part of the school paper. Photography was a particular interest of hers. To be on the staff with Todd made it even better. The room was full as she entered.

Egg McNaughton was telling Tim Anders about the new student teacher's awards and achievements. Tim, a non-athlete, was listening politely.

"Mr. Cartwright was named outstanding athlete in his freshman year. He was captain of the football team and he's won dozens of weight lifting competitions."

Tim was mildly curious. "How do you know?"

"He told me so," Egg announced proudly. "He's a great guy. He's willing to talk about his college career anytime. You should go in there and ask him questions about it."

Tim looked bored. "What if I don't want to know anything?"

Egg looked at his friend in disbelief. "You might want to try weight lifting yourself, Tim. It's a great challenge."

Lexi put her hand over her mouth. She had a hunch that *she* was more interested in weight lifting than Tim Anders. Still, Egg's enthusiasm was difficult to ignore, and Egg himself was impossible to avoid.

On the far side of the room Anna Marie was hanging a bulletin board, ignoring Egg and the lecturing tone he'd taken with Tim about the merits of Cartwright. Lexi crossed the room to where Anna was working. "Hi," she chirped.

"Hi, yourself." Anna Marie kept hanging brightly colored letters with stick pins.

"What are you doing?"

"Mrs. Drummond asked me to arrange the new bulletin board." Anna Marie stepped back and put her hands on her hips. "What do you think?"

"Nice. You have an eye for color. I like it."

Anna Marie looked at Lexi in surprise. "You do? Really?"

"Of course I do. I wouldn't say so if I didn't."

"Thanks."

Lexi studied Anna Marie for a moment. "You sound surprised."

"I guess I'm just not used to people paying me compliments, that's all," Anna Marie said softly, "about anything."

Anna Marie had lost a good deal of weight, Lexi observed. She was actually a very pretty girl. Her eyes had a beautiful, dreamy quality.

Egg's enthusiastic voice interrupted Lexi's thoughts.

"You know, Tim, I really think my work-out schedule would help you. Why don't you come over after school tonight? I'll show you the program I've worked up for myself and I can even give you some of my health recipes. 'You are what you eat,' my mom always says. Do you like tofu? I have the best recipe for a tofu burger. . . ."

As the two boys disappeared through the doorway, Lexi chuckled. "Once Egg gets an idea in his head, it's hard to stop him."

Anna Marie smiled faintly. "I don't know Egg McNaughton very well."

"He's a great guy," Lexi said. "I'm glad he's my friend, even though I am getting a little tired of this body-building kick he's been on. Ever since that Mr. Cartwright came—Coach Derek's new student teacher—Egg hasn't quit talking about him."

"I don't blame him," Anna Marie said softly.

Lexi looked at her with surprise. "Oh? Do you like Mr. Cartwright, too?" she asked.

Anna Marie's expression turned dreamy. Lexi could see a slight smile tilt the corners of her lips. "I think that Mr. Cartwright is probably the most handsome and intelligent teacher we've ever had here at Cedar River. I can't remember ever having one quite like him." She sighed. "It's a shame to waste him on all that dumb coaching stuff."

Lexi studied Anna openly. It was obvious that she had a serious crush on Evan Cartwright. As Lexi listened, Anna Marie continued.

"I wish he were teaching my History class or something, just so I could hear his voice." Then she frowned. "Some of the girls said that he's going to be teaching girl's Phy. Ed. for a few weeks."

Lexi looked at her understandingly. "Does that bother you?"

"I'm no good in Phy. Ed.," Anna Marie said ruefully. "I'm too clumsy. It seems like I'm always the one to strike out or knock a ball out of bounds or shoot one through the wrong hoop." Anna Marie's face looked tight and worried. "I really hate Phy. Ed.!"

Anna was sensitive about her size, Lexi was sure. Everyone in the Phy. Ed. classes at Cedar River was required to wear brief white shorts and colored T-shirts with the words "Cedar River Physical Education Department" printed on the front and back. No one looked particularly attractive in the Phy. Ed. uniforms. For someone sensitive about their weight, the brief shorts could be a real problem. Still, Lexi reminded herself, Anna Marie *was* slimming down.

Lexi glanced at the big pendulum clock on the wall. "Whoops," she gasped. "I'd better get busy and finish typing those captions or I'm going to be late for my next class."

Anna Marie turned back to the bulletin board. By the time Lexi was finished typing, Anna had cleaned up the scraps of colored construction paper and was dumping them into the waste basket.

"It was nice talking to you," Lexi called, as she went out the door. "See you in Phy. Ed."

Lexi could see the worry in Anna Marie's eyes at the mention of Phy. Ed. class.

———

Binky, Jennifer and Egg were already seated at a table by the time Lexi arrived in the lunchroom. She pushed her tray along the metal rails and grabbed a taco and a dish of pudding, then walked across the noisy room to join her friends. She glanced to see what everyone was eating.

"Don't even look at Egg's plate," Binky warned. "He brought his usual weird concoction from home. He may as well have scraped slime off the bottom of the bathtub and put it on a piece of whole wheat bread." Binky made a wretched face, squeezed her eyes shut and stuck out her tongue. Egg ignored her.

Jennifer studied her taco, carefully picking out every bit of diced tomato she could find. Without looking up, she announced, "I don't see how Egg can put some of that stuff in his mouth."

Egg turned to her with a disgruntled look. "It's good for you, that's why. It builds muscles."

"Who says?" Jennifer retorted.

"Coach Derek for one," Egg said. "Phy. Ed. today was great. We played basketball, and Cartwright had some really terrific tips, things some of the guys on the basketball team hadn't even thought about before. Everybody's saying that if he could be our coach, we'd probably take the state championship. Cartwright told us that—"

Binky made a gagging sound. "I'm tired of hearing how wonderful Mr. Cartwright is. He can play basketball. He can play football. He can lift weights. He can read minds. See the man play the piano without his hands ever leaving his wrists. . . ."

"Don't be smart, Binky," Egg said, annoyed. "You don't know him."

"And I'm not sure I want to. I'm tired of hearing how great this guy is."

Lexi smiled to herself, almost enjoying the argument between Binky and Egg. It seemed everyone thought Mr. Cartwright was special in one way or another, especially Egg and Anna Marie.

After lunch, the girls' locker room was abuzz. As Lexi changed clothes, she listened to the conversations around her.

"Mr. Cartwright is *so-ooo* cute," Minda said. She spoke in a shrill, high-pitched voice that was impossible not to hear. The Hi-Fives, a girls' club Minda belonged to, giggled.

"He's got great legs," Tressa observed. "I saw him walking across the gym in his shorts on the way in here."

"Great legs, great arms, great face, great hair," Mary Beth added.

"Maybe Phy. Ed. isn't going to be so bad this

quarter after all." Minda smiled.

The Hi-Fives all giggled again.

A pounding on the locker room door drew their attention. "All right, break it up in there. Let's get out on the floor, it's time to play ball."

There were squeals and shouts as they finished dressing and dashed out of the locker room onto the gymnasium floor to field the basketballs Cartwright was tossing out.

As Lexi warmed up, she thought of her friend Peggy and what a fine basketball player she was. Peggy had gotten pregnant and been sent away by her family to live with her uncle until after the baby was born. The thought made Lexi very thankful that *her* biggest worries were the photo captions for the *River Review*.

Anna Marie was trying to make some lay-ups. It occurred to Lexi then that Anna had reason to worry about Phy. Ed. class. She wasn't a good basketball player.

Anna Marie's expression was tense. While she dribbled the ball awkwardly with one hand, she pulled at the hem of her shorts with the other. It was difficult for her to dribble and to pass. Often she missed the person to whom the pass was intended and the ball flew out of bounds.

"That's enough warm-up," Mr. Cartwright announced. "Number off into teams. Start here. . . ."

Lexi's stomach did a flip-flop when she realized that she, Anna Marie, Minda Hannaford, Tressa and Binky were going to wind up playing on the same team. Lexi usually avoided doing anything in a group with Minda. It always meant trouble. Today, however, Lexi sensed that she wasn't going to be the target of Minda's attention. Minda was already eyeing Anna Marie with disgust.

It took only a few plays to see that Anna Marie froze under the basket. To shoot, she threw the ball wildly into the air. Sometimes it bounced off the backboard, sometimes it flew over the backboard, hitting the wall and rolling to a corner of the gym.

"Can't you do anything right?" Minda shouted. She glared at Anna Marie, her hands on her hips, her legs apart. "Quit shooting air balls! You're losing this game for us."

Lexi put her hand on Minda's arm. "It's just practice, Minda. It doesn't matter. It's only Phy. Ed."

"I don't care," Minda said sharply as she jerked her arm away. "I don't like losing. If she has to play on our team, we're never going to win."

"I'll try harder. I really will," Anna Marie promised. She was close to tears.

"I don't know all the rules," she explained, as she and Lexi ran down the court together.

"You two quit talking out there and start playing ball." Mr. Cartwright was standing at the side of the court with a frown, his hands balled into fists and propped rigidly against his hips. "This isn't a tea party, you know."

Lexi had never seen a Phy. Ed. instructor become so involved in the game. He angered easily, and spent most of his time running up and down the side of the court shouting instructions.

"Who are you guarding?" he yelled, pounding his fists on the wall. "This isn't a birthday party. Get out there! Do your stuff. You're open. You're open. Take a shot, take a shot. Rebound! Can't you see we need the points? Rebound!" Mr. Cartwright's voice echoed through the gymnasium nonstop as he attempted to frighten, cajole or inspire the girls into a frenzied game of basketball.

"You there, Blondie," he barked, pointing a finger at Minda, "quit hogging the ball. Maybe you want to be a star, but I think you'd better let some of your teammates shoot, too."

Minda shot him a daggered look.

Mr. Cartwright's harsh sideline coaching and coarse words were tarnishing the glow of mystery and excitement that had surrounded him. What's more, the girls were getting tired.

"I thought this was Phy. Ed.," someone muttered under her breath, "not a district championship."

"He sure is competitive."

Lexi noticed that Anna Marie was looking terribly flushed, her cheeks a mottled red. Droplets of sweat were pouring from her forehead and her shoulders drooped in a weary position.

"Okay, girls," Cartwright announced, "I'm going to let you do a full-court press now. Let's see how you hold up under pressure."

Anna Marie shot Lexi a panicky glance. Instead of impressing Mr. Cartwright, as she had hoped, she was drawing dirty looks for the blunders she made on the court. It wasn't until the last minute of play, however, that Anna Marie made her fatal error.

They were under the opponent's basket, the score tied. Anna Marie was guarding the opposing team's center, a tall girl with good instinct for the basket. Distracted by a player behind her, Anna Marie turned to look over her shoulder. In a split-second the tall girl put the ball into the basket with a soft swish. The opponent's score increased by two and the buzzer sounded.

Mr. Cartwright's handsome face flushed red. He thrust a pointing finger at Anna Marie. "Hey, Chunky, who were you supposed to be guarding anyway?"

The ten girls on the basketball court were suddenly still, in a state of shock. Even the girls on the bench remained seated, with frozen stares aimed at Cartwright.

Lexi's gaze darted toward Anna Marie who stood awkwardly under the basket, her hands still outstretched in a feeble attempt to stop the ball. The color drained from her face, and her arms dropped slowly to her sides.

Lexi was the first to move. She crossed the court to Anna Marie. "It was a good try, Anna Marie. Good game."

Mr. Cartwright turned away sullenly.

Anna Marie gave Lexi a teary smile. "Thanks, Lex." Together they left the gym floor. Anna Marie held her head high and proud, as if to show the other girls that Mr. Cartwright's cruel comment had not hurt her, but Lexi could see the anguished expression in her eyes.

Why? Lexi wondered. *Why did Mr. Cartwright say such a dumb thing, anyway?*

Chapter Three

"Anna Marie. Wait up!"

It was three forty-five and the hallways were emptying. Anna Marie's shoulders were hunched wearily, as if she were carrying a heavy weight square in the middle of her back. Lexi sensed that the girl shouldn't be alone. She fell in step with her.

"May I walk with you? Jennifer and Binky have disappeared, and Todd has to spend some time talking to Coach Derek this afternoon."

Anna Marie smiled faintly and nodded. "Sure, why not?"

"Where do you live?" Lexi wondered.

Anna Marie gave her address.

"That isn't far from my house! We're practically neighbors. I'm surprised I haven't seen you walking before."

Anna Marie shrugged. "I'm not out very much. I'm usually too busy."

"Oh?" Lexi said, curious. "Do you have an after-school job?"

"No, not exactly." Anna Marie hesitated, as if it

were difficult for her to explain what kept her so busy. "Tonight for example, I'll probably be typing all evening."

"Big paper due?" Lexi asked.

"Not mine. I offered to type Mary Beth Adamson's English paper."

"Why? Aren't you busy enough with your own schoolwork?"

Anna Marie shrugged. "I am. By the time I get Mary Beth's and my own done, it'll probably be two in the morning."

"Then, why. . . ?" Lexi questioned.

"I don't know exactly," Anna Marie admitted sadly. "I just seem to . . . agree to things. Mary Beth asked me. She said she didn't have time to do it herself, and I just said I would."

"Is she paying you?" Lexi asked.

Anna Marie shook her head. "No, she never does."

"Then I don't understand. . . ."

"I like to make people happy, that's all. Mary Beth is always really nice to me when I type for her."

Well, I would be too! Lexi thought to herself indignantly. Mary Beth was using Anna Marie. Couldn't she see that?

"I know you think I'm stupid to do it. I realize it's probably silly, but I can't help it." Anna Marie's voice was self-conscious sounding and distant. "I guess maybe I think it'll make people like me if I do things for them."

"People should like you for who you are. Not for what you do for them. *I* like you and you don't have to type anything for me."

"I think you're the first person who has ever told

me that." Anna Marie scuffed at the dirt with the toe of her sneaker.

Lexi studied Anna as they walked together. She seemed to have lost even more weight. It occurred to Lexi that the reason Anna was so unhappy was not because others didn't like her. The reason she was so unhappy was that she didn't like herself.

"Have you lived in Cedar River all your life?" Lexi asked, after a few moments.

"Most of it. We moved here when I was five." She glanced at Lexi. "Do you like it here?"

"Yes. I thought I'd hate it when I had to leave Grover's Point, and I did for a while. It was tough being the new girl in town, but now I feel like this is where I've belonged all along."

"I've watched you. You're lucky. You seem to fit in."

"If you'd said that to me the first month I was here, I would have laughed in your face," Lexi admitted. "I felt like I didn't fit into Cedar River any better than a round peg fit into a square hole!"

"Really?" Anna Marie looked surprised. "I never would have guessed."

"Minda and I had a little trouble at first," Lexi admitted ruefully. "Minda wasn't exactly an enthusiastic welcoming committee."

"I can sure imagine that easily enough. Minda's not very . . . nice."

"She has that reputation," Lexi said mildly. She didn't like saying things about Minda, even if Minda had been nasty and unreasonable. Lexi knew that somewhere deep inside, there was a decent streak in Minda. Somehow, someday, that nice person might come out and surprise them all.

"Do you have any brothers or sisters?" Anna Marie asked.

"Just one. My little brother, Ben," Lexi said proudly. "He's a great kid. He's almost nine. He goes to the Academy."

Anna Marie's eyebrow arched. "Isn't that a school for the . . . the. . . ."

"The handicapped," Lexi finished for her. "Yes, it is. My brother has Down's syndrome, but he's a great little guy. He's really learning a lot at the Academy."

"Is it hard for him?" Anna Marie wondered curiously.

"School?" Lexi shook her head. "He keeps up and he's made lots of friends. Ben's very outgoing. In fact, he made a friend for me here in Cedar River. I was lonely, and he announced one afternoon that he was going to find a friend. The next thing I knew, he was towing Peggy Madison into our yard."

"That's nice," Anna Marie smiled. "I have a little brother too. I don't think he likes me well enough to go and find any friends, but he's not too bad as little kids go."

"Is he your only brother?" Lexi asked.

"One brother, one sister. My sister's older," Anna Marie answered simply. "We aren't very close. I wish we were." Just then, Anna Marie looked up and pointed toward a large, three-story Victorian house. "Here it is. This is where I live."

"Oh, what a pretty home!" Lexi gasped. "It's—it's huge."

Anna Marie nodded. "Yeah. Huge and old. My dad is a Mr. Fix-It. He likes to tear things apart and rebuild them. He's great at refinishing furniture. That's why he wanted this house. He said it would give him a lifetime hobby."

Lexi looked up at the high-peaked roof. "Two lifetimes, maybe."

Impulsively, Anna Marie asked, "Would you like to come inside?"

"Sure. Why not?"

The girls walked to the back of the house and mounted five steep steps to the entry. Anna Marie's mother was in the kitchen kneading a huge wad of bread dough on the counter.

"Well, hello there," she looked up from her work, her fists still buried deep in the puffy dough. "I see you've brought company, Anna Marie. How nice."

"Hi, Mom. This is Lexi Leighton. She's in my class at school."

"Nice to meet you, Lexi," Mrs. Arnold smiled. "You'll have to excuse me if I don't shake your hand."

"That's all right," Lexi laughed, "I can see you're busy."

The kitchen was a wonderful conglomeration of old and new. There was a cook stove in one corner and on the wall across from it was a huge restaurant range. It was obvious that this was a well-loved, well-used room in the Arnold household.

Lexi took a deep breath. The room smelled of cinnamon, vanilla and chocolate.

"Would you girls like something to eat? I just finished baking three kinds of cookies. There's chocolate chip, sugar, and peanut butter." Mrs. Arnold gestured toward a table in a small, windowed sun-room. "Your brother Ricky is already having a snack; why don't you join him?"

Lexi's gaze traveled to the bright little sun-room with a round oak table and four antique chairs. Ricky was sitting at the table, busily stuffing cookies into his mouth. Lexi's eyes darted back to Mrs. Arnold. She was a plump, jolly woman with shiny red cheeks that looked like apples. Ricky was a miniature version of his mother. He was oblivious to the fact that Anna Marie had a guest, totally engrossed as he was in the cookies he was eating.

"Will you pour me some more milk, Anna Marie?" Ricky asked, extending his glass.

"You could say hello first," Anna Marie chided. "This is my friend, Lexi."

"Hi, Lexi," Ricky said around a mouthful. "Now, will you pour me some milk?"

Lexi burst out laughing. "I guess all nine-year-old brothers are the same. That's exactly what my brother Ben would do."

Ricky looked interested. "You have a brother? Is he in my class?"

Lexi shook her head. "No, Ricky, he's not. My brother Ben goes to the Academy."

"Oh, I know that place," Ricky said cheerfully. "That's where they have the Special Olympics."

Lexi nodded. "Right." It didn't seem to trouble Ricky that it was a school for the handicapped.

"Does your brother have friends?" he inquired curiously.

"Oh, lots of them—at school," Lexi said.

"Do they live near here?" Ricky asked.

"Not so many are around here. Most of the kids that go to the Academy are either driven or bussed in."

"Would he like to be my friend?" Ricky seemed genuinely interested in getting to know Ben.

Mrs. Arnold had freed herself from the bread dough and walked toward the table, wiping her hands on a towel. "Ricky's best friend just moved away and he's feeling rather lonesome," she explained. "He's hoping to find some new friends in the neighborhood."

"Why don't you come over sometime," Lexi invited, "and meet Ben for yourself. He's a very nice boy. He's also very good at putting puzzles together. Do you like to do puzzles?"

"Only if they're trucks or dinosaurs," Ricky said frankly.

"Well, then you and Ben should get along just fine. He must have half a dozen dinosaur puzzles."

"All right." Ricky pushed the cookie plate away. Just then the telephone rang, and Ricky made a dive for it. He took the cordless telephone and darted out of the room, leaving Mrs. Arnold shaking her head.

"You'll have to excuse Ricky. He's very outgoing, but he's also a very typical nine-year-old. No manners, unless reminded."

Anna Marie took two cans of soda from the refrigerator and handed one to Lexi. Though both were the same flavor, one was diet, and Anna kept that one for herself.

"Help yourself to cookies if you like," she said.

"Aren't you going to have one, too, Anna Marie?" her mother asked.

She shook her head. "Nope. All I want for now is this soft drink. Is Dad home?"

"He's in the living room," Mrs. Arnold said, nodding toward the doorway. "Why don't you go in and say hello?"

The girls walked together into the large, high-ceilinged living room.

"Dad, I'd like you to meet my new friend. This is Lexi Leighton," Anna Marie said.

Mr. Arnold stood up and shook hands with Lexi. "Welcome to our home, Lexi."

"You have a very beautiful house," Lexi said.

"Why, thank you. Has Anna Marie told you about my restoration project?" With that, Mr. Arnold launched into a long, detailed explanation of what he was doing to the woodwork in the house to bring it back to its original beauty.

Deftly, Anna Marie interrupted him. "Dad, I'm not sure Lexi wants to know *everything* you're telling her."

Mr. Arnold blushed faintly. "You're absolutely right, Anna Marie. I tend to get too involved in my projects." He headed for the door, excusing himself, and smelled the aroma from the kitchen. "Right now, I think I'll sample your mother's bread. How does that sound to you?"

Both girls smiled as Mr. Arnold left the room.

"He's very nice," Lexi said after he left.

Anna Marie nodded. "My dad's a great guy. I wish he were home more. He's usually on the road; he's a salesman. It's not often he's home from work when I get here."

"Maybe I should go," Lexi offered. "You'd probably like to spend some time with him."

"That's all right. He's going to be here all week."

Lexi noticed a family photo on the piano.

"That's my entire family, including my mother's brothers and sisters," Anna Marie explained.

Everyone in the picture appeared overweight except Mr. Arnold. All his wife's family had her apple-cheeked look. Then Lexi noticed one dark-haired, slim girl in the back row of the picture.

Anna Marie pointed to her at the same moment. "This is my older sister. Look at her. She's so skinny!"

It was true. Compared to the rest of the family, the girl looked very thin, almost out of place.

"I don't know how she got to be so scrawny and I got to be so . . . fat!"

Mr. Arnold strolled into the room and peered over the girls' shoulders at the photo on the piano. "There's Anna Marie," he pointed out, "and that's my tiny one." He pointed to the thin girl at the back. "She's in college now. We miss her, don't we honey?" Just then his wife called from the kitchen and he was gone again.

Lexi looked at Anna Marie and was surprised at the distressed expression on her face.

"You'd think he'd call *me* his tiny one, wouldn't you?" she said indignantly. "I *am* the youngest." Anna Marie looked down at herself disgusted and smoothed her blouse. "Of course, I'm not *tiny* like her. But I certainly don't need everyone to keep pointing that out."

"Anna Marie," Lexi began, "is what Mr. Cartwright said in Phy. Ed. class still bothering you?"

Anna Marie's lips pursed in a pout. "No! I don't even want to think about him. Mr. Cartwright was rude and he was cruel."

"Well, I agree with that," Lexi said honestly. "Plus, it's untrue."

"Tell me what it's like to be in the Emerald Tones," Anna Marie asked brightly, changing the subject. "I haven't known too many people who are part of that group."

"It's great. Mrs. Waverly is a super director, and the music she selects for the group is really fun. Some of it's hard, but when we pull together and get it right, we even impress ourselves! A photographer came from the local paper this week. We're going to be written up in the daily news."

"I'm impressed," Anna Marie said with a smile. "Maybe someday I'll be able to say, 'Oh, I knew the Emerald Tones before they became famous and went to Hollywood.' "

Lexi laughed. "I think the closest thing you'll be able to say is 'Oh, I knew the Emerald Tones before they graduated and went to college.' By the way, did you know that the school paper *River Review* is up for an award?"

"Really?" Anna Marie asked, her eyes lighting with interest.

"A professional communicators group has decided to give awards to outstanding high school newspapers. Todd Winston's name and mine were even mentioned for the photos we took. How about that?"

Lexi noticed that Anna Marie was easy to talk to—open, warm, friendly, interested in just about everything that was going on at the school. The two of them talked quite awhile about the teachers they'd shared.

Suddenly, out of the blue, Anna Marie said, "Do you know who I think is a great guy?"

"Who?" Lexi asked curiously.

"Matt Windsor. Did you know that he's started going to the library every Saturday morning to participate in a reading program for kids there?"

"Really?" Lexi's eyes widened with interest.

"He reads to preschoolers. Can you imagine?" Anna Marie laughed delightedly. "Matt Windsor, with his black hair and tough-guy looks, sitting on the floor reading *Dr. Seuss* to little tiny kids. I love it."

"That sounds like Matt," Lexi said chuckling.

"At first the children were scared of him, because sometimes he wears a black leather jacket. A couple of them even started to cry. Now he's the favorite reader at the library—they all love him. I know all this because my mother is a friend of the librarian."

The two girls talked for a long time—giggling, comparing notes, debating the merits of various types of lip gloss. Suddenly, the huge, old grandfather clock in the hallway began to chime the hour. *Bong! Bong! Bong. . . .*

"Six o'clock!" Lexi yelped, jumping from her chair. "My mother will wonder where in the world I am. I was enjoying myself so much, I forgot to call home."

"I enjoyed it too, Lexi. I'm glad you walked home with me. I hope you'll come again."

"Next time, why don't you come to my house?" Lexi suggested as she headed for the door. "Goodbye, Mr. and Mrs. Arnold," she called, "I'm glad I met you."

"You too, dear," Anna's mother called after her.

Lexi walked quickly toward her home. The

thoughts in her mind raced with her steps. There was more going on inside Anna Marie Arnold than people might realize. She was an intelligent, sensitive girl. She was also hurting. Lexi wondered what she could do to help her heal.

Chapter Four

Lexi was glad to be home. Although the Arnold household was pleasant, her own home felt warmer, more welcoming.

"Lexi, do you want to stir this gravy while I mash the potatoes for supper?" Mrs. Leighton, who had a dusting of flour on her apron, checked the pan. "Oh, dear, never mind. It looks like it's already done. I'll have to put it on low while I cut the meat."

"Where are Dad and Ben?"

"They're in the living room watching TV. Ben has this new fascination for wrestling."

"When did that start?" Lexi wondered.

"Who knows where Ben comes up with these things? Both of my children are constantly surprising me." Mrs. Leighton smiled.

Lexi wandered into the living room where her father was seated on the couch, his feet propped against a footstool. He was reading the daily paper.

Ben was positioned in front of the television set, his eyes riveted to the screen. As Lexi watched, he flung himself to the floor with a loud grunt and began executing his version of the wrestlers' moves. He groaned and moaned and flipped back and forth across the floor, his arm locked around an invisible neck, his heels digging into the carpet.

"Uh . . . Ugh . . . Oooff . . . Gotcha! I've got 'em Dad, in a headlock," Ben yelped. "See me? See me?"

"I certainly do, Ben. Now that you've got him, what are you going to do with him?"

Ben flung his arms open wide and rolled across the floor. "Let him go," he said logically. "I'm a wrestler, Lexi. Aren't I good?"

"Truly excellent, Ben," Lexi said with a laugh. "Where'd you learn to do that?"

Ben pointed solemnly toward the television. "Every Tuesday," he said. "Want to wrestle with me, Lexi?"

"I don't think so." Lexi shook her head. "You look too tough for me."

"Too tough," Ben echoed. "Ben's too tough for Lexi."

"Right now, you'd better go upstairs and wash up for dinner. Mom's ready to cut the meat."

"Too tough," Ben repeated, "Too tough. Ben's a tough guy," as he meandered out the door and up the stairs.

Shaking her head, Lexi sat down by her father. "What are you going to do about that boy, Dad?" she asked playfully.

Mr. Leighton chuckled. "Stay out of his way? I think Ben is too tough for his old father, too."

Lexi settled back against the cushions of the sofa and glanced at the television. Wrestling was over and the next sporting event was about to begin.

"Now it's weight lifters," Mr. Leighton commented. "Look at the size of those guys."

Lexi stared at the screen as massive men with bulging, bulky muscles paraded onto the stage. Mr. Leighton watched intently too, shaking his head. "All I can say is that sports have certainly changed since I was young."

"How's that, Dad?"

"Look at those guys! Those can't be natural muscles."

Lexi looked again at the screen and then at her father. "What do you mean?"

Mr. Leighton wrinkled his brow and pursed his lips.

"Muscles aren't like new cars, Dad. You can't just go out and buy them," Lexi reasoned.

"In a way you can," Leighton said. "Of course, as a medical professional, I can't approve of it." He caught Lexi's confused expression. "I'm talking about steroids, honey."

"Steroids?" Lexi echoed.

"Steroids are drugs, Lexi. Drugs used by athletes to make their muscles develop faster, making them stronger, more energetic."

"If drugs can do that, why doesn't everyone take them?"

"That would be a good question, Lexi, if you didn't know about the down side of taking steroids, the bad things that can happen."

"Bad things?"

"When an athlete first starts taking steroids, everything seems to go his way. He gets larger and stronger. His endurance becomes much greater and he has a winning edge. The problem is that steroids affect the body in a lot of ways that aren't so positive."

"Like what?" Lexi asked, still thinking steroids sounded like a pretty good idea.

"Well, for one thing, they can kill you."

Lexi's eyes widened.

Just then Mrs. Leighton called everyone to supper. Though the conversation around the table turned to other things, Lexi had a hard time forgetting about the discussion she'd had with her father about the use of steroids. After the dishes were cleared, and her mother was getting Ben ready for bed, Lexi sought out her dad again in the living room.

Mr. Leighton laid down his newspaper. "Maybe I should explain this a little better. Steroids are actually 'anabolic steroids.' The word anabolic means 'body-building.' Lots of athletes, and sometimes even their coaches and doctors believe it's worthwhile to use steroids because they increase the body's muscle and reduce fat at the same time."

"Every athlete does this?" Lexi asked in amazement.

"Oh no, not at all. All athletes aren't involved in sports where steroids would be to their advantage. Only body-builders and weight lifters need that kind of size and strength. Some runners may take them for endurance. They think they can get it quickly with chemicals. Someone who plays tennis or racquetball or even baseball really doesn't need steroids, because they're counting on their skill at hitting the ball and maneuvering around the court or field to win the game. When an athlete is competing in an arena that requires sheer strength or endurance, many are tempted to try drugs to enhance their own natural strength."

"I've never heard of steroids before," Lexi admitted.

"Well, I'm glad their use hasn't filtered down to Cedar River yet. I was just reading a study that said steroids were becoming a severe problem in colleges and even in some high schools."

"You mean even a young kid could take them and develop muscles that big?" Lexi stared again at the weight lifters posturing on the screen.

"Young people have been known to take them. The irony is that steroids in young people could permanently stunt their growth."

"That's awful."

"And that's not the worst of it. Steroids are very hard on a person's kidneys and heart. I'd guess that people who use steroids are shortening their life span by several months or possibly even years."

"Then why do people use them? I don't understand."

"Because they want that extra edge, Lexi. They want to compete and they want to have the advantage over their opponents."

"So they'd take something that could kill them?" Lexi said in disbelief.

"Some athletes are so desperate to win, so desperate to reach a goal, that they'll do just about anything to achieve it, refusing to acknowledge that anything negative can come of it. It is the nature of steroids not to have negative side effects immediately. At first, all that happens is positive. The individual fills out, gets stronger, acquires more energy. It's only later that they discover the bad side effects."

"Yuck, I don't think I want to watch weight lifting on TV anymore."

Mr. Leighton smiled. "I'm not suggesting that every athlete takes steroids, Lexi. I'm just saying it's a problem, and I suspect not everyone in that group we just saw is drug-free."

"Can't the authorities test for it or something?" Lexi asked.

"They can and they do," Mr. Leighton replied. "But there are ways around being found out." He stood up and put his arm around his daughter. "Just don't come home tomorrow and announce that you're taking up weight lifting, Lexi."

Lexi laughed and gave her father a quick hug. "Don't worry. I don't even like carrying a laundry basket full of clothes! I don't think weight lifting is for me."

Mr. Leighton's expression became serious.

"Is something wrong, Dad?"

"Oh, I was just thinking about a friend of mine from the town I grew up in. His name was Gwinner."

"What about him?" Lexi asked. "Did he use steroids?"

Mr. Leighton nodded. "It was a long time ago when steroids weren't even considered a dangerous drug. Gwinner wanted to be the biggest guy at the gym, so he used to pop the drug like candy."

"What happened to him, Dad? Is he still alive?"

Mr. Leighton's expression was sad and he shook

his head. "Frankly I don't know, Lexi, but I doubt it."

"What makes you say that?"

"Well, the last time I visited your grandpa and grandma, I went to see Gwinner. He was sitting behind a desk, laughing and joking as he had for as long as I've known him. But he looked like a skeleton. Instead of the husky, healthy-looking man he had been, he was frail, small, and very old looking. His skin was a bleached white and thin like parchment paper. You could see his veins and bones right through." Mr. Leighton shook his head sadly. "It just about killed me to see him like that, Lexi."

"What had happened to him?"

"He told me he was on kidney dialysis then, and would be for the rest of his life. Although he didn't say it, I think he knew his life wasn't going to last much longer."

"How terrible! Why don't they ban steroids?"

"Well, it's not that simple, Lexi," Mr. Leighton explained. "Steroids are a medicine as well, and for some people, they are very necessary and very helpful. It's just like any other medicine—it should only be taken when you have an illness that requires it. In other words, they should never be taken just to make yourself more fit or muscular for sports. I especially hate to see young people tampering with these things. Who would want to risk a heart attack, high blood pressure or sterility as a teenager? It's a strange society we live in, when winning is so important that we're willing to lose everything that really matters just to experience that occasional win."

"You're scaring me, Dad."

Mr. Leighton gave his daughter a hug again. "I'm sorry, Lexi. Even though I'm a veterinarian, I am a doctor. I don't like to see suffering, especially when it's unnecessary. Taking steroids can cause that. I'm really sorry if I got carried away and scared you."

Lexi thought again about the athletes she'd seen on television. The weight lifters' powerful muscles didn't seem nearly so healthy or attractive anymore.

———

On Saturday morning, Ben woke Lexi with an excited shout, dashing into her bedroom and flinging himself across her bed. "Ben's getting company," he said with delight. "Hear me, Lexi? Ben's getting company." He put the palms of his hands on either side of Lexi's cheeks and rolled her head back and forth across the pillow.

Lexi groaned and opened one eye. "What time is it?"

"Who'd come over on a Saturday morning? Don't they know that's when people sleep late?"

Ben flip-flopped like a fish out of water on the bed. "Don't you want to know who Ben's company is?" he demanded.

"All right, who is he?" Lexi asked with a yawn. "Somebody from the Academy, I suppose."

"Nope. Ben's new friend."

Lexi opened her eyes a little wider. "You have a new friend, Ben?"

He nodded smugly. "Ben's new friend is coming over. Ricky's coming over."

"Ricky Arnold?" Lexi said. She was suddenly wide awake.

"Ben's friend Ricky is coming." He squirmed off the bed and landed with a small thud on the floor. "Ricky's coming soon."

"When did you get to know Ricky?" Lexi asked.

"He came to see me after school," he explained. "We're friends."

Ricky Arnold had been true to his word. He'd said he would like to meet Ben and now he was coming to visit. That pleased Lexi a great deal. It was nice to know that not everyone was afraid of a child with Down's syndrome. She hoped Ben and Ricky would have a good time this morning.

The door bell rang and Ben shot out of the room with a delighted squeal. "My friend is here. My friend is here," he yelled as he clambered down the stairs.

By the time Lexi had showered and dressed, Ben and Ricky were sitting in the living room at a table working on a huge dinosaur puzzle. Though Ben had many problems and learning disabilities, he was very clever at putting puzzles together and had an unerring eye for fitting just the right piece into an unexpected spot.

Ricky's face was screwed into a concentrated frown. He and Ben were placing puzzle pieces with one hand and eating popcorn out of a large bowl with the other.

Lexi rode her bike to her father's office to do the chores that she usually did on Saturday and returned home just before lunch. Ricky and Ben were already sitting at the table and Mrs. Leighton was ladling homemade soup into their bowls.

"Ricky's staying for lunch," Ben announced with pleasure.

"Yeah," Ricky said nodding and eyeing the table, "and this looks great."

Mrs. Leighton had made sandwiches with home-made bread and had also set out a plate of freshly baked German chocolate cake.

Lexi smiled, knowing how much Ricky loved to eat.

"You're going to join us, aren't you Lexi?" Mrs. Leighton asked.

Lexi washed her hands in the kitchen sink and sat down at the table. "Of course I am. It looks great! What kind of soup is it?"

"Beef barley," her mother said as she dished up a bowl for Lexi.

"You're a good cook, Mrs. Leighton," Ricky announced after five minutes of concentrated eating.

"Why, thank you, Ricky. You're a good guest."

Ricky grinned, his apple-cheeks gleaming. "It's more fun eating here than at home."

"More fun?" Lexi asked.

"Yeah. Anna Marie used to be more fun," he said sourly, reaching for another sandwich. "But she's not any fun at all anymore."

"Why is that?" Lexi asked, surprised. Anna Marie had become much more friendly in the past few days and Lexi was growing to like the girl very much.

Ricky shrugged. "She's just boring, that's all. Really boring."

"All little brothers think their big sisters are bor-ing," Lexi pointed out.

Ricky shook his head. "Not like Anna Marie. She's always exercising."

"Exercising?" Anna Marie was certainly not ath-letic. It was surprising to hear that exercise was such a big part of her day.

"Yeah, she must do a thousand sit-ups a day."

"A thousand sit-ups!" Ben echoed.

Ricky nodded emphatically. "Maybe two thou-sand!"

"Two thousand," Ben echoed.

"Yeah, it could even be three thousand sit-ups a day. She's *always* exercising."

That seemed very unlike the Anna Marie Lexi was getting to know.

"Could I have some cake now, Mrs. Leighton?" Ricky asked eagerly. "It looks really good."

"Help yourself, Ricky."

Lexi passed the plate to him, spearing a piece of cake for herself as she did so.

Ricky stared at her dumfounded. "Are you really going to eat that?"

Lexi looked at the cake and then at Ricky. "Sure I am. Why not?"

Ricky smiled faintly. "I was just wondering. Anna Marie never eats cake. In fact, she never eats period."

Mrs. Leighton chuckled. "Well, that's a pretty strong statement, Ricky. Don't you mean Anna Marie doesn't eat much?"

"No. Anna Marie never eats." He looked from Mrs. Leighton's puzzled expression to Lexi's. "She's getting weird, you know," he said matter-of-factly.

"She sits up to the table with us, but she never eats. I caught her once. She pretends to eat, but then feeds it to the dog."

Mrs. Leighton and Lexi both stared at Ricky. He nodded knowingly.

"Our old dog McMutt lies down right by Anna Marie's chair while we're eating. She puts the food in her lap and hands it to him. Come on over to our house and just see how fat McMutt has gotten. Then you'll believe me."

"That's very odd," Lexi said. "I wonder why Anna Marie's doing that. . . ."

"You think that's weird," Ricky said with a snort, "you should see what I found in the flower pot the other day."

Now even Ben was staring at his new friend curiously. "In the flower pot?"

"It was Dad's birthday on Thursday," Ricky explained, "and Mom made him a pan of fudge. Since it was her special fudge, Dad offered some to everyone. I found Anna Marie's in the flower pot."

A little snuffle of giggles distracted Lexi. Ben had his hand over his mouth. "Fudge in the flower pot," he chanted. "Feed the doggy dinner." He giggled again. "Ricky, your sister's funny."

"I think she's funny, all right. She's just plain *weird*. I don't care if she eats or not. I just wish she and Mom would quit arguing about it."

Ben, who occasionally latched onto a phrase that struck him, was still chanting, "Fudge in the flower pot, fudge in the flower pot."

Mrs. Leighton rose from her chair. "Maybe we should change the subject, kids. How about it?"

"Fudge in the flower pot, fudge in the flower pot."

Mrs. Leighton passed the plate of cake again to Ricky and Ben, and they both began talking of other things. But Lexi could not forget what Anna Marie's little brother had told them.

Chapter Five

Lexi met Anna Marie in the school hallway. "I'm on my way to the cafeteria," Lexi said. "Harry and Binky are going to save a table for Jennifer, Todd and me. Would you like to join us?"

Anna Marie looked doubtful. It was as though she was having a difficult time deciding whether she dared join Lexi and her friends.

"Oh, come on," Lexi encouraged. "They'll be glad to have you."

"Are you sure?" Anna Marie said. "I don't want to intrude."

"In the lunchroom?" Lexi said with a laugh. "You won't be intruding. Come on!"

She grabbed Anna Marie's elbow and steered her toward the cafeteria, afraid that if she let go, Anna Marie might dart away.

"I'm sure hungry today, aren't you?" Lexi said as she filled her tray from the selection in front of them. She took chicken nuggets and french fries, a piece of fruit and a carton of chocolate milk. Lexi glanced back to see that Anna Marie had one slice of white

53

bread and an orange on her tray.

"Is that all you're eating?" she blurted.

Anna Marie frowned. "I'm not hungry. I had a big breakfast."

That's doubtful, Lexi thought to herself. Anna Marie was looking thinner every day. Her cheeks even looked sunken. Still, Lexi didn't comment about it. She could see her friends waving them over from a table across the room.

Anna Marie followed Lexi to the table. As she put her tray down, Lexi announced, "Anna Marie's going to join us today."

"Great," Harry said. "Move over, Binky, so she can sit down."

"Hi, Anna Marie," Todd greeted her.

Jennifer gave a little wave of her hand and a friendly smile. Though Lexi's friends had welcomed Anna Marie warmly, the girl remained quiet and unsmiling.

When Anna Marie returned to the lunch line to pick up a carton of milk, Jennifer leaned toward Lexi with a frown and muttered, "What's wrong with her?"

"What do you mean?" Lexi said.

"Doesn't she know how to smile? She looks like she lost her best friend."

"Oh, just ignore that," Lexi said. "She doesn't know you guys very well yet. She doesn't have a lot of friends."

"Well, I know it's hard for people to get used to me," Jennifer said pointedly. "But she doesn't have to look so glum."

When Anna Marie returned with her milk, Lexi's

head was bowed in a short prayer. When she looked up, Anna Marie was peeling the orange and breaking it into sections. Then she methodically broke the sections into yet smaller pieces and scattered them about her plate. Lexi wondered if she'd taken even a single bite.

Without comment, Lexi began eating her own meal. Occasionally, she'd glance at Anna Marie. She noticed that when the orange was broken into as many tiny pieces as Anna Marie could manage, she started on the bread. Discreetly, she crumbled pieces of the bread into the napkin in her lap and carefully folded over the corners. When most of the bread was gone, Lexi watched Anna Marie crumple the napkin tightly into a ball and lay it on the side of her plate. Anna Marie had managed to visit casually through the entire meal and not put more than a crumb or two of food into her mouth.

No one except Lexi seemed to notice the girl's strange behavior.

Harry glanced over his shoulder with a puzzled frown. "I wonder where Egg is. He said he was coming for lunch."

Binky gave a disgusted sigh and stabbed her fork into the banana on her plate. "He's probably hanging around Mr. Cartwright's office waiting for more words of wisdom. You'd think gold coins were falling from his mouth from the way Egg stands there totally engrossed."

"You wouldn't be mad at your darling brother, would you, Binky?" Jennifer asked craftily. "Do I hear just a little bit of sarcasm in your voice?" she teased.

"Egg's been a real jerk lately. And I thought he was bad before. Now he's absolutely hopeless."

"What do you mean by that?" Todd asked, looking amused. Binky and Egg's sibling disagreements were familiar to them all.

"Oh," Binky huffed, "he can't quit talking about how great Mr. Cartwright is. 'Mr. Cartwright this,' 'Mr. Cartwright that,' 'Mr. Cartwright says,' 'Mr. Cartwright does.' I think Egg would move right into Mr. Cartwright's apartment and sit at his feet day and night if he could. I'm so sick of hearing about Mr. Cartwright I could just choke." Binky's face flushed pink. "Egg thinks Mr. Cartwright knows more than anyone else in the whole world about sports."

"Well," Harry said matter-of-factly, "he *has* won a lot of awards."

"Big deal," Binky said gruffly. "He may have won a lot of awards, but he likes to talk about them, too."

"Todd," Harry said, talking over the top of Binky's head. "Did you hear that Mr. Cartwright was named most valuable player in his senior year of high school? From what I understand, he came from a big school, too."

"Actually, I thought the weight lifting thing was more interesting," Todd pointed out. "There aren't a lot of weight lifters that young who do as well as Cartwright did."

Suddenly, the conversation that began with Binky's complaint turned into an animated discussion of the merits of weight lifting. Abruptly, Todd turned to Binky and asked, "Is Egg still lifting weights?"

"Of course," Binky replied disgustingly.

"And still eating health food?" Todd asked with a smile.

"Yeah. Have you guys ever seen uncooked tofu? My mother was so grossed out by it she made Egg keep it in a non-see-through container. I think he's losing some interest in it. Besides, he doesn't have time to fool with his diet anymore."

"Why is that?" Todd looked puzzled. "I didn't know Egg had taken on any new jobs."

"Oh, he hasn't. No new job—except Mr. Cartwright, that is."

"He's working for Mr. Cartwright?"

Binky shook her head. "No, no. He just spends all his time with him. He doesn't have time to fix his food or work out. He just wants to hang around and hear what the man has to say. It's as if he could get his strength by—" Binky stammered for a minute, searching for the word, "osmosis, or something!"

"Osmosis!" Todd yelped. "Binky McNaughton, when did you start using such big words?"

Binky blushed as Todd began to tease her. "Osmosis isn't such a big word," she said with as much dignity as she could muster. "It just means to absorb something from the outside—automatically."

"Well, whoopee," Harry said. "Does Egg think he can get all Mr. Cartwright's smarts into his own head if he just hangs around him long enough?"

"Something like that."

Todd burst out laughing. "You must have just come from science class, Binky."

She grinned. "How'd you guess? Still, I think it's true. It's like Egg wants to learn everything that Mr. Cartwright knows about body-building and weight lifting. But he's with him so much he doesn't do his own body-building. It's crazy, if you ask me."

Binky's tirade was interrupted when Minda sashayed by the table. Jennifer stared at the girl for a long moment after Minda went by. "She's showing off," Jennifer commented.

"What's she showing off?" Harry asked blankly. "I didn't see anything different about her."

"That's because you're a man," Jennifer said, disgustedly. "Can't you see? Minda's lost a few pounds. And she wants everyone to know how good she looks. Why else would she walk up and down the aisles in the cafeteria?"

"Because her apple fell off her tray and rolled on the floor and she's looking for it?" Harry said, teasingly.

"Ha!" Jennifer snorted. "She just wants to show off what great willpower she has, and wants everyone to admire how good she looks in her clothes."

Anna Marie moved nervously on the bench next to Lexi and a strange expression crossed her face.

Lexi sensed that something was troubling her—something in their conversation about Minda's diet, no doubt. Unfortunately, before Lexi could ask what was bothering her, the bell rang and everyone dashed to their next class.

"Are you ready to go shopping?" Jennifer asked as she met Lexi after school. "Mrs. Waverly wants us to get our new black skirts to go with our Emerald Tone jackets right away."

"Dad said I didn't have to go to the clinic this

afternoon." Lexi patted the pocket of her jean jacket, "And he gave me some money, too. If I can't find a skirt I like, I'm going to buy the fabric and make it myself."

"Do you have time for that—" Jennifer began, but was interrupted by Anna Marie's appearance in the doorway.

"On your way home, Anna Marie?" Lexi asked.

The girl nodded, and Lexi noted how tired she looked. Anna Marie never seemed particularly happy, but lately, she seemed depressed. Impulsively, Lexi said, "Jennifer and I are going shopping for new skirts for the Emerald Tones concert. Would you like to come along?"

Anna Marie considered it for a moment. "That would be fun, but . . . no, I'd better not."

"Why not?" Lexi persisted. "You could help us pick something out."

"I don't have any money," Anna Marie said, pressing her hands into her jacket pockets. "I'm flat broke."

"That's nothing new," Jennifer said. "I'm always broke. If I don't get to the mall tonight and buy that skirt, I'll be in trouble."

"Think of this as a pleasure trip." Lexi prodded. "You don't need any money."

"You really don't mind?" Anna Marie said.

"Of course not. Come on. If we don't hurry, we're going to miss the bus to the mall."

The wind ruffled their hair as the three girls walked toward the city bus stop. As they waited, Evan Cartwright came driving by in his red sports car. The top was down, the radio blaring and the wind was parting his gold-blond hair.

Jennifer watched intently as he passed. "He really is incredibly handsome, isn't he?" she said, a bit of awe in her voice. "Like a movie star or something. In the teen magazines the guys don't look one bit better than Mr. Cartwright."

"I don't think you're supposed to be thinking about a teacher like that," Lexi teased, knowing full well that every girl in school was drooling over the handsome student teacher.

When Lexi glanced at Anna, she was staring off in the distance with a dreamy look on her face.

If she was thinking of Mr. Cartwright, Lexi was surprised. She'd assumed that the afternoon he'd made such a fool of her in Phy. Ed. class would convince Anna Marie that there was nothing to admire in the man.

The bus arrived before Lexi could make any comment.

The mall was busy and it took some time to get to the store that Mrs. Waverly had recommended. They pulled several black skirts off the rack and took them back to a large dressing room with a three-way mirror.

In addition to the black skirts, Jennifer found two or three brightly colored sweaters and Lexi spotted a pair of jeans. Anna Marie also found some clothing she wanted to try on. The three girls hurried into the dressing room, giggling.

"This large room is great," Jennifer commented. "This way we can all be together." She hung the new clothes on a hook and started to pull off her sweatshirt. "Actually, I could stand to inherit a million dollars just to buy myself a new wardrobe."

"That would be some wardrobe if you spent a million dollars on it," Lexi commented as she tugged the jeans over her hips. "I'm so glad you don't ever exaggerate, Jennifer."

Jennifer grinned and pulled a sweater over her head. "How do you like this neon green sweater I picked out?"

"You look like something from the frozen foods department," Lexi said, sticking out her tongue.

Jennifer admired the bright sweater in the mirror and began to dance around the dressing room. "Maybe I'll start a new trend, dressing like brightly colored foods. My red T-shirt could be my strawberry shirt—or cherry."

"Or tomato," Lexi added. "If anyone can get away with wearing bright colors, you can, Jennifer."

The girls were giggling and teasing, oblivious to Anna Marie standing before the three-way mirror in her underwear, staring at her slimmer body. Lexi was shocked to see just how much weight the girl had lost.

"What are you doing?" Lexi asked, "Aren't you going to try anything on?"

"Oh, I'm just looking at this horrible body," Anna Marie sighed.

"It certainly doesn't look horrible to me," Lexi pointed out. "You have really lost a lot of weight." She didn't add that she thought Anna Marie might even be too thin for her large frame.

"Well, Lexi, you need glasses," Anna swung around, staring then at her backside in the mirror. "Yuck." It doesn't take glasses to see how flabby my thighs are," Anna Marie patted at her legs. "And my stomach," she groaned.

Lexi stared at Anna Marie in surprise. She was anything but flabby. In fact, Anna Marie was actually pleasant-looking, if a little thin. Lexi stood next to her in the mirror.

"I may even weigh more than you do now, Anna Marie. How do I look?"

Anna Marie was startled at the question. "Why, you're beautiful, Lexi. You always have been."

"I don't know about that," said Lexi, "but I think we both look nice, Anna Marie. You shouldn't be so hard on yourself. You're being unrealistic. And you're *not* too heavy."

"I hate my body, Lexi," Anna groaned. "I really do."

Lexi was silent for a moment before she asked, "Anna Marie, have you ever heard of 1 Corinthians 3:16?"

The girl looked blank. "No. What's that?"

"Well, it's a verse in the Bible that says, 'Don't you know that you yourselves are God's temple and that God's Spirit lives in you?' "

"And what is that supposed to mean?" Anna Marie asked somewhat indignantly.

"It means a lot of things, actually, but basically it means that our bodies are temples made by God in which He wants to dwell. He considers them beautiful. He wants us to see them that way too. We should treat our bodies as temples of God."

Anna Marie stared at Lexi scornfully. "I don't know what you're talking about, Lexi, but if our bodies are temples, God's got some pretty bizarre ones."

Chapter Six

It was ten AM the next Saturday when Todd arrived at the Leighton's door dressed in blue jeans and a plain T-shirt.

"Todd Winston reporting for duty." He grinned and gave a snappy salute. "The kitchen patrol has arrived."

Lexi invited him into the house with a wave of her hand. "You're just in time. I've laid out all the ingredients."

Every now and then, the two of them spent a Saturday morning in the Leighton kitchen pulling taffy, making cookies or cakes, or—as they were doing today—making a triple batch of fudge. When they finished, they would take the freshly made cakes or candies to the home for the elderly four blocks away and distribute them to the residents.

Lexi had long ago come to the conclusion that it was she and Todd, not the elderly residents, who were getting the most benefit from the activity. Giving out small gifts and visiting with people starved for attention made Lexi and Todd feel wonderful inside.

Her mother always said that it was better to give than to receive. Lexi had never truly understood that concept until they'd started these trips to the home.

Todd, who was as familiar with the Leighton kitchen as Lexi was, began to pull heavy saucepans out of the cupboard. "Do you think we can keep three kettles of fudge going at once?" he asked. "Remember how easily it scorches."

"We'll need another pair of hands," Lexi said.

"Here's Ben's hands," Ben announced from the doorway. "Ben can cook."

Lexi and Todd looked at each other doubtfully. Ben had helped them "cook" before. Usually it ended in disaster.

"Why not?" Todd shrugged his shoulders. "One of these times it's got to work out."

Lexi nodded. "All right, Ben. You can stir. Can you handle that?"

"Ben can stir," he affirmed. "Ben can do anything."

"That's the spirit, little guy," Todd smiled. "Push that chair over here beside me and hike up here. Let's get started."

———

About an hour and a half later, Todd confessed, "You were right, Ben, you *can* do anything." He put an arm around the boy's shoulders. "Would you like to come to the home with us and deliver the fudge?"

Ben nodded enthusiastically, then jumped up and down. "Ben will come. Ben can cook," he announced.

"Okay, let's just tear off some pieces of aluminum foil so we can package the fudge as soon as it's cool," Lexi said.

Just then there was a frantic knocking at the back door.

Lexi hurried to open it and found Binky standing there, her face pale, her expression troubled.

"Binky, come in!" Lexi led her by the arm into the kitchen. "Are you all right?"

"You look like you've just seen a ghost," Todd added.

"You and Harry didn't have a fight?" Lexi wondered.

"No, no. Harry's fine. At least I think he is. I haven't seen him all day. But this isn't about Harry," she said, her voice high-pitched and nervous sounding. She pulled a stool to the counter and sat down. "Can I have a glass of water? I feel funny."

"You aren't going to faint?" Todd asked.

"What happened?" Lexi was getting impatient.

"Actually, I don't quite know." Binky was calming down. "I'm not sure I can figure out what happened."

"Well, tell us what you can. Maybe we can help you," Todd encouraged.

Lexi went to the sink for a glass of water for Binky.

"I got up this morning and couldn't decide what to wear," Binky began. "Nothing so unusual. Actually, I wanted to wear something black because I'd bought these new black barrettes for my hair and—"

"Get on with it," Todd prodded.

Binky threw him a disgusted glance. "This is important to my story. You'll have to hear me out. Anyway, I didn't have any black T-shirts, but I remembered that my brother Egg had one. You know, the one with the University emblem on it? I thought I could borrow it so I could wear my new barrettes."

Todd rolled his eyes in exasperation.

"Well, I went looking for Egg and couldn't find him," Binky continued, "so, I just went into his room and started looking for the T-shirt."

Ben, who'd been silent until now, chimed in. "Lexi doesn't like me looking around in her room."

Binky grimaced. "Well, apparently Egg didn't like it either, because all of a sudden he appeared in the doorway and started screaming at me."

"Egg? Screaming?" Todd asked in disbelief. "That doesn't sound like him at all."

Binky's eyes filled with tears. "He's *never* talked to me that way before. He's never been that angry with me. I know that we fight sometimes, but this was different—his face turned red, almost purple, and his eyes narrowed and he looked mean . . . really mean. He was furious with me. He said that I was a snoop and that I had no business going into his bedroom. He wanted to know what I was doing going through his dresser drawers. Then he asked how I'd like it if he came into my room without permission and started pulling things out of my drawers. He said that if I ever did anything like that again, he was going to tell Mom and Dad and have me grounded for the rest of my life."

Lexi's eyes widened and she blinked. "I'd say Egg was over-reacting."

"For the rest of your life?" Ben echoed, his little

mouth hanging open in amazement. "Binky's gotta stay home for the rest of her life?"

Lexi busily piled some fudge onto a plate and handed it to Ben. "Here Ben, take this fudge to Dad. See if he thinks it's okay. You can have some, too."

Ben trotted eagerly toward the living room.

"Sorry about the interruption," Lexi said. "Sometimes I forget how big little ears can be."

"Did he say anything else?" Todd asked.

Binky's eyes filled with tears. "He said he hated me. He said he wished I wasn't his sister and that he didn't have any family to go snooping around in his room and his things and. . . ." Binky started to sob.

Lexi looked at Todd questioningly. "I'm sure he didn't mean those things, Binky. That doesn't sound like Egg at all."

Todd shook his head in agreement. "That's not the Egg that we know, Binky. Something must be wrong. What could be his problem?"

"I don't know," Binky wailed. "I can't figure him out anymore. He's like a—a stranger to me."

"A stranger? What do you mean?" Lexi asked.

"He's so secretive. He doesn't talk to me anymore. He doesn't tell me anything. He doesn't tell me what he's doing or what he's thinking. Egg and I used to fight, but at least we talked. I don't feel like he's my friend anymore."

Todd frowned, worried by this turn of events. "How long has this been going on, Binky?"

"He's been different ever since he started lifting weights, trying to impress Minda Hannaford. Things have gotten a lot worse lately, ever since—" Binky's eyes lit up with the realization. "Ever since the new student teacher, Mr. Evan Cartwright, came to Cedar River High School.

"They've become such good buddies, that it seems like Mr. Cartwright has even replaced our family. Egg gets up extra early in the morning so he can get his exercising done and be at school in time to visit with Mr. Cartwright. After school he doesn't come home right away. He hangs around to see if he can erase blackboards or run errands for him. Then he spends the whole evening quoting what he said! I'm *sick* of Mr. Cartwright," Binky concluded angrily.

Then she began to cry. Tears slipped from beneath her tightly closed eyelids; then a gulping, choking sob seemed to well up from inside her. When Binky opened her eyes, they were pools of tears.

"Sometimes Egg and I may appear as if we really hate each other. But we don't. Not at all. We just enjoy the conflict sometimes." Binky took a raspy breath. "I love my brother and I always thought he loved me . . . until now."

Todd put his arm around Binky's narrow shoulders, giving her a comforting squeeze. "Don't do this to yourself, Binky. Don't cry anymore. I'm sure Egg loves you. Whatever's going on with him has nothing to do with you. You just temporarily got in his way, that's all."

"But I was in his . . . (sob) . . . room."

"True, but you've gone into his bedroom before, haven't you?"

"All the time," Binky said.

"And you've borrowed his clothes before, haven't you?"

"Of course."

"Well then, why should today be any different? Why don't I talk to Egg to see if I can find out what's going on," Todd offered. "Maybe it's, you know, guy stuff. Something he'd rather talk to me about than you."

"You'd do that?" Binky said, looking hopeful. "You'd see if you could find out why Egg is so mad at me?"

"Well, frankly, I don't think he's mad at you," Todd said. "I think he's mad at something else and just took it out on you."

Binky shuddered. "Well, I certainly don't ever want to be in his way again if that's what's going to happen."

Todd squeezed her again. "I'll see if I can find Egg right now. We can deliver that fudge to the rest home later, can't we, Lexi?"

"Of course. Binky can help me wrap it and we'll just put it in the fridge until you come back."

Todd nodded and smiled. "All right. See you later then," and he retreated out the back door.

"Todd's a great guy," Binky said with a snuffle as she reached for tissue.

"Egg's a great guy, too," Lexi assured her. "Don't worry about him anymore. Let Todd take care of it."

Binky nodded uncertainly, but she began to help Lexi wrap the fudge. They were just stacking the last of the packages when the doorbell rang. Lexi looked up to see Anna Marie standing on the doorstep, and she asked her in.

"You're just in time," Lexi smiled. "Binky and I just finished packaging some fudge for the rest home and we've got a whole plate of scraps here for ourselves."

"Scraps?"

Lexi nodded. "Yeah. You know, the end pieces, the ones that got cut too small or crooked. There's always something left from our baking and cooking projects to sample." Lexi gestured toward the plate. "Help yourself."

Anna Marie took a step backward and shook her head. "No thanks. I don't care for any." Then she patted her stomach and said, "I'm stuffed. Really."

Lexi was surprised. Anna Marie had lost so much weight lately that she could hardly believe she could be stuffed. She never saw her eating anything. In the school cafeteria she always seemed to be playing with her food, rearranging it on the plate but never putting any of it in her mouth.

"Are you sure?" Lexi said. "It's really excellent fudge."

"That's for sure," Binky said enthusiastically, as she reached for another piece.

Anna Marie got a stubborn look on her face. "I don't want any. I'm not hungry." Then, rather than sit down and join in conversation with the girls, she picked up a magazine and started to thumb absently through its pages.

Lexi and Binky continued to sample the fudge. "Milk anyone?" Lexi asked.

Binky nodded. "This stuff's pretty sweet. You need something to wash it down," she admitted.

Anna Marie shook her head. "No, thanks." She continued to leaf through the magazine. "This just drives me crazy," she finally said, snapping the pages with frustration.

"What makes you crazy?" Binky asked curiously,

looking over her shoulder at the magazine.

"These advertisements. The magazines are full of them. If it isn't a food product to buy, it's a recipe."

"Yeah, I guess you're right." Lexi joined Binky to peer over Anna Marie's shoulder.

Anna Marie held up the cover of the magazine which pictured a huge piece of strawberry shortcake. "Look at this mess."

"Looks great to me," Binky said. "I love strawberries and cream."

"What's wrong with it?" Lexi asked.

"Well, they depict this huge, fattening dessert on the cover, and then look at the titles of the articles inside." Anna Marie ran her finger down the list of contents. " 'Walk Your Way to Thinness,' 'The Glamour Diet,' 'How to Lose Weight While Dining in the World's Finest Restaurants.' And look at this one! 'Is Your Puppy Obese?' Don't you see what I mean?"

Lexi and Binky shrugged. "It's pretty normal, I guess," Lexi acknowledged.

"They tell you it's unhealthy to be fat, that you shouldn't eat too much, and then on the next page they give you a recipe for the rich dessert on the cover." Anna Marie whined.

Binky studied the magazine. "You're right, Anna Marie. It is pretty silly, isn't it?"

Lexi thought about it for a moment. Anna Marie was talking about getting mixed messages.

"It's the same thing in my family," Anna Marie continued. "Every time I go to my Aunt Josie's, she gets her feelings hurt if everyone doesn't clean their plate."

"Yeah, my grandma's like that," Binky said.

"But does your grandma greet you at the door with 'My, my, aren't you gaining a little weight? Are you going to be chubby like your mother?'" Anna Marie's expression showed her confusion and anger. "What does she want from me? To clean up my plate or starve to avoid being like my mother?" Anna Marie crumpled the magazine and tossed it aside. "It really upsets me. I just get so tired of it all!"

Lexi and Binky exchanged glances. What a day! First Egg, now Anna Marie.

"Say, Lexi," Anna Marie asked, her voice back to normal. "Where did you get that fudge recipe?"

"From my mom. It was her mother's recipe. It's been in our family a long time."

"Do you think I could borrow it? My dad loves fudge. Maybe I could make him a different kind for a surprise."

"Sure," Lexi said. "I don't mind a bit. I'll copy it down for you and bring it to school."

"That would be great," Anna Marie smiled. "I've been doing a lot of cooking at home lately. My mom likes to get out of the kitchen once in a while, and my dad likes big meals."

"You cook big meals at home?" Binky asked with surprise. "After the conversation we just had, you could have fooled me."

"It's just a . . . thing . . . I've gotten into lately. I've even started a recipe file. I'll add Lexi's fudge to that."

"Why don't I copy it down for you right now?" Lexi went to the cupboard for a recipe card and a pen. As she wrote, it occurred to Lexi that Anna Marie was oddly interested in food, while refusing to eat it.

Why would anyone want to think about and read about food all the time and not want to taste it? Lexi finished writing out the card and handed it to Anna Marie. "I hope your family likes it."

"I'm sure they will." Anna Marie stood up. "I'd better go. I didn't realize what time it was."

"Oh, what're you doing this morning?" Binky wondered.

"I've started jogging five miles a day," Anna Marie answered.

Binky whistled through her teeth. "Five miles a day! Wow! I'm impressed."

Anna Marie shrugged. "It's not so much, really. It goes pretty fast. I'm building up my endurance. In fact, I'm thinking of raising it to seven miles. Maybe I'll start today."

Anna Marie started to jog lightly in place to warm up. Then she dropped her hands to the floor to stretch. "I'd better get going if I'm going to get my seven miles in. Thanks for the recipe, Lexi. I'll let you know how it turns out."

As Anna Marie left the kitchen, Binky and Lexi stared at each other and shook their heads.

Chapter Seven

After church on Sunday morning, Lexi and Ben stopped at the rest home to deliver the fudge. Lexi hadn't heard from Todd since he'd left the afternoon before to speak to Egg.

Ben, who loved to be the center of attention, was a big hit at the rest home, handing out packages of fudge and visiting with the residents. Lexi felt uneasy. This was something she and Todd had always done together and it seemed strange to be here without him.

Ben, however, was doing an excellent job of endearing himself to dozens of people with his sweet smile and loving expression. "All done, Lexi," Ben finally announced. "No more fudge."

"We'd better go home now, Ben. Mom said we'd have a late lunch."

Ben nodded excitedly, always eager to have lunch.

Lexi tried to hide her concern from her little brother. Ben wouldn't understand what was going on with her friends. She could hardly blame him. Lexi couldn't understand it herself.

It was nearly three o'clock when Todd finally arrived at the Leighton home. His expression was grim, his blue eyes seemed overcast with grey.

"Can I come in?" he asked, sounding preoccupied.

"Of course," Lexi said. Her mother and father were upstairs taking an afternoon nap. Ben was busy in the kitchen arranging and rearranging the buttons from his button box. "Let's go into the living room. We can be alone there."

When they reached the room, Lexi turned suddenly to face him. "What's wrong, Todd?"

"I'm sorry I didn't get back here to help you deliver the fudge," Todd apologized.

"It's all right. Ben and I did it today after church." Lexi smiled faintly. "If you aren't careful, he's going to take away your job. The people at the home loved him."

Todd sat down wearily on the couch. Lexi stood impatiently in front of him. "Well?"

He sighed and stared at the ceiling. Then he restlessly ran his fingers through his hair, pulling it to the back of his head. "I talked to Egg."

"And?" Lexi could see Todd was very hesitant.

"I don't know if it's something I can repeat to you."

"Why?" Lexi asked, plopping down on the couch next to him. "Did Egg ask you not to?"

"Not exactly," Todd said. His voice was tired and flat, unlike his normal tone, or anything like Lexi'd heard before. Lexi felt a spiral of alarm in her midsection. "But he told me some things that are, well, awfully private."

"Of course I don't want to intrude on Egg's private life, but I do want to know if there's something I can do to help," Lexi said. "He and Binky are two of my very best friends in the world and I can't stand to see this rift between them."

Todd finally relented. "I guess I can talk to you, Lexi. I should know you can keep a secret."

"Of course I can," Lexi assured him.

"When I left here yesterday afternoon, I went directly over to the McNaughtons'."

Lexi nodded. "Yes."

"Egg was in the basement, lifting weights."

"Mmm," Lexi smiled. "That seems to be about all he does lately, isn't it? Lift weights and mix protein drinks."

"He didn't seem happy to see me at first," Todd went on. "I think he sensed that I might be up to something. Anyway, I asked him what had been troubling him lately."

"What did he say to that?"

"Well, at first, he said 'nothing.' He told me my imagination was getting carried away. Then I told him that Binky and I had been to your place, and I explained how upset she'd been. He was sorry to hear that Binky had been crying. He admitted he'd been pretty hard on her and said he planned to apologize."

"Did he tell you *why* he was so angry?"

"Not really. He just said that he'd had a lot on his mind. He added, almost as an afterthought, that he really didn't want anyone snooping in his dresser drawers in case they found something that they shouldn't."

"Something? Like what?"

"He wouldn't tell me. He just wanted to talk about weight lifting. Then finally he got around to asking the question that really shook me up." He paused.

"What question, Todd?"

"Egg asked me if I thought it was all right to take 'stuff' to help him get stronger."

"Stuff?" Lexi echoed. "Like vitamins?"

Todd's expression was strained. "No. Stuff that Mr. Cartwright had given him—some drugs that he'd gotten in college from his own weight lifting coach."

"You mean, that's why Egg was so angry? He was afraid Binky would find it?"

"That's my guess," Todd nodded.

Lexi thought for a moment, and suddenly it was all very clear. She remembered the muscle builders on TV that she'd seen with her father. "Steroids?" she gasped. "You mean Mr. Cartwright gave Egg steroids?" It was hard to believe that Egg would do something so stupid.

The expression on Todd's face told her otherwise. Steroids were exactly what they were talking about. If Binky had found the drugs and told her parents, Egg would have been in deep trouble. No wonder he'd been so upset!

"Todd, are you sure it was Mr. Cartwright who gave Egg the steroids?"

Todd dropped his gaze and stared at the ends of his fingers as if being silent would make the subject go away.

"But Evan Cartwright is a teacher!" Lexi exclaimed. "Why would a man in that position give one of his students drugs? Isn't that wrong?"

"According to Egg, Mr. Cartwright told him that lots of weight lifters in college take them, and it really helps their performance. He offered to help Egg build up his body quickly to impress Minda. He said he could give him some steroids to help him get started."

"You mean Egg is already taking them?"

Todd shook his head. "Not yet. He had the pills hidden inside a new pack of tube socks in his dresser. That's why it blew his mind when he walked into his room and found Binky digging in his sock drawer."

Todd went on, "Egg said Mr. Cartwright told him that he'd noticed a big difference in his physical appearance. He said it shouldn't take too long, and he understood how impatient Egg was."

"Well, according to my dad, steroids are really dangerous," Lexi said. She told Todd about the television program, and how distressed her father was that anyone would abuse their body in that way.

"I don't know much about this, Lexi," Todd admitted. "I've heard about guys that have taken them. Now there's all the talk about drug-testing in the Olympics, but I don't actually know what effect steroids have on the body." He glanced at his watch. "Do you have plans for the rest of the afternoon?"

Lexi nodded her head. "Sort of. I've got a Bible study I'd like to finish for next Sunday, and then I promised Ben that I'd do a puzzle with him."

"Just wondered if you'd like to go to the library with me—to look up steroids."

Lexi went to the hall closet. "Sure, for a while. Let me grab a jacket and tell my parents where I'm going."

Todd was already waiting in his blue '49 Ford Coupe. Lexi slipped into the passenger seat without comment. Neither spoke until they reached the parking lot of the Cedar River Public Library.

Lexi had always loved libraries. She enjoyed wandering through the rows and rows of books, imagining all the years of research, imagination, even sweat and tears that had gone into creating the volumes that surrounded her. Today, she had the foreboding thought that she might find out something she didn't want to learn.

"Are we crazy?" Lexi asked, as she stared ahead at the large wooden doors of the library.

Todd took her elbow and gently guided her toward the door. "We have to do this, Lexi. If Egg is into something dangerous, we need to know about it. We're his friends. The only way we can help him is to know what we're dealing with."

Lexi drew a deep breath and they mounted the stairs together.

The librarian at the reference desk looked up and smiled when they approached. "May I help you?" she whispered.

Lexi glanced around to see several people studying at long tables.

"We need to do some research on a certain topic," Todd explained. "Can you help us?"

"What is it you'd like information about?"

"Steroids," he said simply. Lexi winced, and looked around to see if anyone had heard. Her stomach began to churn a little.

The librarian did not seem surprised or uncomfortable with the request. She jotted down several notes on a slip of paper. "I recommend you start with a subject index. Here are some other suggestions that might help you in your search. If you have any questions, please come back to me."

Todd tucked the paper into his shirt pocket. Then he tugged Lexi's fingers gently. "Come on. Let's start over here."

It took them a half hour to gather material from the sources the librarian had suggested. Todd and Lexi each took an armload of books to an empty, sound-proof study room. They dumped the books on the table and Todd shut the door.

"At least we can talk more freely in here," he said. "All this tiptoeing around makes me feel guilty, like we're doing something wrong."

Lexi looked bewilderedly at the stack of books. "Looks to me like we've just made a lot of work for ourselves."

They divided the information between them and began to read. After a while of intense study, Lexi spoke up. "Some of this is pretty complicated. These are medical books. Most people take drugs when they're sick. Athletes sometimes take drugs . . . painkillers, vitamin supplements, even steroids, in order to perform better."

Todd frowned. "Sounds to me like athletes are awfully desperate to win at whatever they're doing. Some athletes take more vitamins than their body can handle or pop painkillers when they should probably be going to a hospital." He shook his head. "And I always thought playing sports was a healthy thing to do."

"It can be," Lexi observed. "It's just that some

people make it an obsession and begin to hurt themselves."

"Like Egg?"

"I wish he could understand what he's going to
do to himself if he gets into this steroid thing," Lexi
said. "We only have one body. If we spoil it, we can't
stand in line for another one."

Todd whistled between his teeth. He looked as if
he were on the verge of being sick. "If Egg could read
some of this, I think he'd change his mind in a hurry."

Lexi listened intently.

"It says here that when the hormone balance is
upset in the body it has a hard time fighting off dis-
eases, particularly cancer."

"Cancer? That's serious."

"You bet it is. It says that a disrupted hormone
balance can cause the growth of cancers."

Lexi was reminded that her family had lost one
of their closest and dearest friends to cancer back in
Grover's Point. It had been a sad time for everyone.
Why would anyone purposely take drugs and risk
that kind of danger?

"Since all steroids have to be processed through
the liver, it is one of the body organs that steroids
affect the most," Todd read on. "I want to be a doctor,
Lexi," he added, "but it would really be hard on me
to find this in any of my patients."

He continued to read aloud. "Steroids, apart from
being the cause of all sorts of liver disorders, including hepatitis, can also cause problems for the kidneys, and promote heart disease. Open heart surgery
is more common in athletes who have taken steroids
when they were young."

Lexi gasped. "According to this article, athletes who take steroids when they're young could be dead within ten to fifteen years from heart attack or cancer. Even the lucky ones are going to have problems. There is even a risk in bearing children, because the genes have been tampered with.

"Of course, the stories we're reading cite the worst examples," Lexi pointed out. "After all, Egg's only sixteen years old. He's not going to gulp these things down like the athletes the medical books are referring to."

"I don't know, Lexi. I don't know how desperate Egg is to change himself. And I don't know how much of a dosage it takes to harm your body. I suppose it's different for every person. What I can't understand is why Egg wants to do it at all."

Lexi was quiet awhile before quoting the passage that was on her mind. " 'Don't you know that you yourselves are God's temple and that God's Spirit lives in you? If anyone destroys God's temple, God will destroy him; for God's temple is sacred, and you are that temple.' "

Todd looked at Lexi, as if unsure of her point.

"Don't you see? Egg doesn't view his body as God's temple. Egg doesn't see that his body is worthy of his respect and care."

"I think that Egg doesn't have any self-esteem because Minda looks through him instead of at him," Todd said frankly.

"We're not just talking about self-esteem here, Todd. We're talking about loving ourselves and caring for ourselves because God created us."

"I suppose you're right, but how many teenagers

do you know, Lexi, really, that have a whole lot of self-esteem? Kids that really think they have some value?"

"Not many, I suppose," Lexi admitted. "It's tough being a teenager. All I know is that God created me and He created you. He created everyone in Cedar River, and the world, for that matter, and He still thinks we're each one of a kind. I believe that's what makes us special—not because of anything that we do or say or inherit from our parents, but because God made us. I don't think Egg—or anyone—should tamper with God's creation."

"You're pretty convincing," Todd said, "but when you're sixteen, it's still hard to believe."

"I know. My mom and I have talked about having respect for yourself and not letting anyone talk you into doing something that you feel is wrong. Mom says God only wants good for us, not harm, and that it's our job to just say 'no' to things that will hurt us."

"Have you got any ideas on how we can convince Egg of this?"

Lexi shook her head. "All Egg cares about is the fact that Minda doesn't like him and he wants to make her notice him. The awful part is that Mr. Cartwright is telling him that he can have whatever he wants if he takes these drugs."

"He's desperate, Lexi. What's more important to Egg right now? The respect of Minda and Mr. Cartwright, or some disease that he may or may not get twenty years from now?"

With a sinking sensation in the pit of her stomach, Lexi knew that Todd was right.

"Todd," she said sincerely, "I'm scared. Egg could really hurt himself if he goes ahead with this."

"I know that, Lexi," Todd agreed. "I'm scared, too. But I don't think he's done anything yet. At least he says he hasn't. I'm hoping he's more nervous about it than he'll admit. It's a good thing, too, or he'd probably already have the stuff in his system."

Lexi chewed on the end of her pencil. "This temple of God verse has been coming to my mind all week, and it hasn't been because of Egg, at least not until today."

"Oh?" Todd looked curious. "Who were you thinking of?"

"Anna Marie Arnold. She's got me worried too."

Todd was beginning to looked discouraged. "I think we'd better start praying for our friends, Lexi. It's the least we can do, and maybe the best thing."

Chapter Eight

"If I eat one more thing, I'm going to explode," Jennifer said as she sprawled across her bed looking at the ceiling. "You'll have to pick the pieces off the walls."

"Oh gross," Binky said, wrinkling her nose and reaching for another brownie. "Quit talking like that, you're ruining my appetite."

"Nothing could ruin her appetite," Lexi confided to Anna Marie.

In two hours, they'd managed to devour two plates of nachos, a bag of chips and dip, a pan of brownies, and part of the pizza that had just been delivered.

Binky jumped up to change the music on the compact disc player. "This is great, Jennifer," she said excitedly. "It's been ages since I've been to a slumber party, especially with this much good food." As she spoke, she plucked a piece of pepperoni from the pizza on Jennifer's dresser. "This is a real pig-out."

Lexi was about to open her mouth when Binky pointed an accusing finger at her and said, "Don't you dare say it, Lexi Leighton."

Lexi looked blank. "What? What was I going to say?"

"Oh, something about speaking for myself."

Lexi laughed. "Actually, I was going to say, 'Pass the chips.' I'm not planning to eat for the rest of the weekend. I think I've about had my quota of food."

"Oh, all right then." Binky's eyes narrowed in mock seriousness. "It's just that you're so much more disciplined than me."

Lexi took a bag of chips and a dish of dip and moved toward the corner of the room where Anna Marie was working out. "Chips, Anna?" she asked, holding up the bag.

Anna Marie shook her head. "No. Thanks anyway, but I'm not hungry." She was on the floor in a leotard and tights doing leg lifts. Before that she'd done stretches, windmills and angry cats.

"Aren't you getting tired of all that?" Lexi asked. "You've been exercising all evening."

Anna Marie glanced at her watch. "Not quite. Give me another ten minutes and I'll be done."

"Are you sure? How long will that be total, then?"

"An hour and a half," Anna Marie said, sweat dripping off her forehead and onto her cheeks.

Lexi squatted down beside the girl and looked at her pink face. "*Why* are you doing this, Anna Marie?" Lexi asked. "An hour and a half of exercise *every* night?"

"Morning and night," Anna Marie corrected as she increased her pace. "I'm feeling really fat again, and I think this will help."

Feeling fat? Lexi was incredulous. She could practically see Anna's ribs through her leotard. Lexi had never seen anyone lose weight as fast as Anna Marie had. How could she possibly think she was still fat?

While the girl continued to exercise, Binky and Jennifer practiced applying mascara to one another's eyes. Lexi went to the far corner of the room and curled up on the bed. She needed some time alone to think. Something was terribly wrong.

Recently, Lexi's free time had been taken up thinking about Egg and his problem. She and Todd had prayed together about what they could do for him. Though the situation surrounding Egg and Mr. Cartwright was frightening, it was a wonderful experience for Todd and Lexi to pray together. According to Todd, Egg was still insisting that he hadn't taken any of the drugs.

Lexi and Todd both wanted to believe that. Unfortunately, Mr. Cartwright's influence over Egg seemed to be growing stronger every day. Todd had admitted that Egg might be lying to him.

Binky had told Lexi that Egg admired Mr. Cartwright so much that he'd do anything in the world for him. What made it so much worse was that the steroid pills promised exactly what Egg wanted. Muscles. It seemed ironic that what Anna Marie wanted was the exact opposite. To be slim.

Binky turned the music up a notch. "I've got a great idea! Lexi, you do Jennifer's hair, while Jennifer does my nails. We can start a little assembly line. Then, Jennifer can do my hair while I do Lexi's nails and," Binky glanced at Anna Marie, "maybe by then, she'll be done exercising and can join us."

Jennifer did a little dance around the room. "No,

I've got a better idea," she said. "Anna Marie's been exercising ever since she got here. Maybe she knows something we don't." She dropped to the floor and started doing leg lifts.

Binky, never wanting to be left out of anything, burst into frantic flopping, doing her version of windmills.

"This is crazy," Lexi announced with a laugh. "But after all the stuff I've eaten, it might not hurt." She turned up the music and joined her friends.

After ten minutes, Jennifer rolled over on the floor on her back and let out a loud groan. "Stop! Stop the music. I can't take it anymore."

Binky dropped on the floor beside her. "How do you keep on with that, Anna Marie? I'm whipped."

Anna Marie ignored them all, intent on finishing the exercise routine she'd started.

"Come on, Anna Marie," Jennifer said, finally. "You're no fun at all. Call it quits."

"Oh, all right. You guys are making it impossible for me."

"You've been at it for almost two hours," Binky pointed out. "You're turning into an exercise fanatic."

"Well, if you can't leave me alone, I guess I'll have to quit," Anna Marie said. She tried to joke, but Lexi heard the irritation in her voice.

Why would anyone want to exercise like that? Lexi didn't understand.

Anna Marie rolled to her hands and knees and started to rise. Lexi saw her falter as she stood up.

"Here, let me help you." Lexi put out her hand to steady her friend.

"Oh," she gasped, blinking rapidly. "I think I stood up too fast. I'm a little dizzy."

"It's no wonder," Binky said with disdain. "All that exercising would make anyone diz—"

Horrified, the girls watched Anna Marie crumple in a heap on the floor.

"She's fainted!" Jennifer shouted.

"Get her some water," Binky yelped, and reached for the nearest bottle of cola.

"Not that," Lexi pushed it away. She knelt beside Anna placing her hands to her cheeks, slapping them gently. "Anna Marie. Anna Marie. Can you hear me? Can you hear me?"

Finally Jennifer stood up. "My mom's downstairs with our neighbor, Mrs. Crawford—she's a nurse. I'll be right back."

Jennifer bolted out the door and clambered down the stairs. In a moment she was back with her mother and Mrs. Crawford, a small, brisk-looking woman with short brown hair and snapping blue eyes.

"In here, Mrs. Crawford. We think she's just fainted."

"Not *just* fainted," Binky stammered, half crying. "It was all that exercise. It had to be."

"What kind of exercise?" Mrs. Crawford looked puzzled. "What have you girls been doing?"

"Well, Anna Marie exercises all the time. She's been at it for almost two hours—ever since we got here," Lexi explained.

"Whatever for?" the nurse wondered.

"She wants to be thin," Jennifer responded.

"So she exercised for two hours?" Mrs. Crawford

was already on her knees beside the girl, lifting an eyelid to check for pupil dilation. "I can't *imagine* why anyone would want to exercise for two hours, unless they were training for something."

"Actually, I think there's more to the problem than just exercise," Lexi conceded.

Mrs. Crawford looked up at her. "What do you mean?"

"I think she fainted because she hasn't eaten."

The woman looked knowingly at Anna's slim form. "Oh, dear," she said, shaking her head.

"You girls had enough food here to feed an army!" Jennifer's mother pointed out.

"But Anna Marie would never eat any of that food," Binky explained. "She used to be real heavy, but she's managed to starve herself into being thin."

"I think you'd better call this girl's parents," Mrs. Crawford told Mrs. Golden. "There is a serious problem here."

The girls all looked at each other, finally acknowledging that their friend was ill.

Then, Anna Marie began to stir. She groaned and put her hand to her forehead. "Ohhh, what happened?"

"You fainted," Binky declared, kneeling beside her.

"How do you feel?" Lexi asked with concern.

Mrs. Crawford helped her to a sitting position. "Who are you?" Anna Marie asked, confused at seeing a stranger in the room.

"I'm Jennifer's next-door neighbor," she explained. "I just happen to be a nurse, and Jennifer called me when you fainted."

"I—I didn't mean to faint," Anna Marie said. "I must have exercised a little too long. They told me to quit."

"When was the last time you ate something, Anna?" Mrs. Crawford asked, matter-of-factly.

"Huh? Oh, well, uh, what time is it?" she stammered.

"It's nine o'clock."

"Oh, I had something at noon."

"You didn't eat any lunch with us," Binky chimed in. "You took a sandwich, but I saw you crumple it up and wrap it in your napkin."

"Oh, I ate some of it," Anna Marie said, worry in her voice. "You just didn't notice."

Lexi remained silent. She had intentionally watched Anna Marie at lunch today. No more than three or four small bites had gone into her mouth, the rest had been wrapped in her napkin as Binky said.

"Well, I'm not a doctor, but my diagnosis, young lady, is that you've had too much exercise and too little to eat today. I think you should have a talk with your parents and get this straightened out."

"But I don't want to leave," Anna Marie protested. "We're having a great time. I'll be fine now. Just give me a couple of those nachos and—"

Mrs. Golden returned to the room. "I just talked to your parents, Anna Marie. They'll be right over."

"No!" the girl protested, her face becoming even more pale. "I don't want to leave. I'm all right."

"I think it would be best if you went home, Anna," the nurse insisted. "You really don't look very well. Just rest here a few moments, and I'll speak to your parents when they come, if you don't mind."

Anna Marie looked frightened. Lexi sat beside her on the bed. "It's all right, Anna Marie. We'll have another slumber party soon. Maybe next week at my house. How does that sound?"

Anna Marie tried to smile, but the tears were coming now. When her parents arrived, she was sobbing, still protesting that she didn't want to leave.

Her mother gently led her to the car and her father helped her in. When they had driven away, Binky, Lexi and Jennifer stood on the steps in dismay.

"Well," Jennifer said finally, "some party this is turning out to be."

The threesome walked slowly back to Jennifer's bedroom, passing Mrs. Golden and Mrs. Crawford who talked in hushed tones in the living room.

"What do you think of it?" Jennifer asked no one in particular when they'd reached her upstairs bedroom.

"I guess that's what happens when you exercise for two hours and don't eat," Binky concluded.

"I'm not surprised she fainted. What surprises me is that it didn't happen sooner," Lexi said bluntly.

"It reminds me of some girls I've known who took ballet lessons," Jennifer said. "They were always dieting too, afraid of gaining an extra pound, afraid of not looking good on the stage." Jennifer reached for a slice of pizza. "I've known girls to go absolutely crazy about dieting just to get a part."

"Well," Binky added gloomily, "this is beginning to remind me of my brother Egg."

Lexi and Jennifer both turned to her with new understanding.

"He's just as obsessed with his body as Anna Marie is with hers. The only difference is that Egg wants to build his body up and Anna Marie seems to want to tear hers down. I think they're both sick." Binky sounded frustrated, almost angry. Suddenly, tears appeared in her eyes. "They both scare me, and I don't know what to do about it. I feel like they're both just slipping away from reality."

Lexi put her arm around her friend. She wished there were something she could say that would make Binky feel better. Unfortunately, the words wouldn't come. Worse, she was afraid that Binky was right. Egg and Anna Marie *were* slipping away and they were helpless to stop it.

———

Anna Marie wasn't in school on Monday or Tuesday. By Tuesday afternoon, Lexi was so worried that after her last class, she slipped out of school without talking to anyone, and walked to Anna Marie's house.

Anna's mother met Lexi at the door. Her cheeks didn't seem as rosy today. "Come on in, Lexi. Anna Marie is in the living room."

"Is it okay if she has visitors?" Lexi asked.

"Oh, yes. I'm so glad you came, Lexi," Mrs. Arnold assured her. "I hope it helps."

Lexi tiptoed toward the living room. Anna Marie was sitting in a large overstuffed chair in front of the television, bundled from head to foot in a thick wool blanket.

"Hi," Lexi said cheerfully.

"Hi yourself, friend." Anna Marie managed a faint smile. "Come on in."

"Are you watching something good on television?" Lexi asked, realizing as she spoke that the sound wasn't on.

Anna Marie shook her head. "No, not really." She sounded wistful and distracted. "How's school?"

"All right, I guess. It would have been better if you'd been there," Lexi smiled. "Are you cold?"

Anna Marie tucked the blanket a little more closely around her. "I'm cold a lot. The doctor says it's because I'm too thin. There's no insulation to keep me warm." Anna Marie's mouth distorted a little, and Lexi thought she was going to cry. "Funny, isn't it? They used to call me Miss Porky, Flap-Flap Thighs, Banana Anna. Now I'm too thin? It's hard to comprehend."

"Do you know what's wrong, Anna?" Lexi asked. "I've been really worried about you ever since the other night at Jennifer's. And when you weren't in school, I thought I should come and see what's up."

"My folks took me to a clinic for an evaluation," Anna Marie said flatly. "That's why I wasn't in school."

"And? What did they say?"

"The doctors diagnosed me as anorexic."

"Anorexic?" Lexi echoed. It was not familiar to her.

"He says I'm trying to starve myself so that I can be thin. The doctors say it's dangerous."

"How dangerous?" Lexi asked bluntly.

Anna Marie just stared back at her for a moment

before answering, "He said I could die if I don't start eating."

Lexi felt like she'd been kicked in the stomach. "Why are you doing this, Anna Marie? Why?"

Anna Marie shrugged her shoulders. "The doctor says that I have to go for counseling. And if I don't start gaining weight, he wants to put me in the hospital."

"How could this happen? I don't understand."

"You really care about me, don't you?" Anna Marie looked intently at Lexi.

Lexi nodded. "I haven't known you for very long, Anna Marie, but I like you very much. And yes, I do care."

"I honestly don't think this would have happened if Mr. Cartwright hadn't embarrassed me in front of everyone in Phy. Ed. class."

The day was vivid in Lexi's mind.

"I was so stupid, Lexi. I had such a crush on him. I thought he was the most handsome man I'd ever seen in my whole life. For some dumb reason, I thought maybe he'd like me, too. Then when I made a fool of myself in that game, and he called everyone's attention to it, I realized that I wasn't pretty or smart or attractive. I was just fat and dumpy. Even the little dieting I'd already started wasn't helping. I was still Banana Anna. Nobody else."

"But Anna—" Lexi began.

She shook her head. "I looked around at everyone who was popular and they were all thin. You, Minda, the Hi-Fives. No one ever calls you names. Life isn't very easy for a fat girl, Lexi. I thought that if I slimmed down my life would be perfect, like yours."

"My life isn't perfect, Anna Marie," Lexi protested.

"It's a lot more perfect than mine," she retorted. "I guess deep down inside, I thought I could show everyone who teased me—Mr. Cartwright, Minda, everyone—that there was really a thin person inside of me." Anna Marie shifted uneasily beneath the thick blanket. "I just wanted to be in control for once, that's all. Can you understand that?"

"I certainly can. When I first moved to Cedar River, I felt like everything was out of control in my life."

"What did you do about it?" Anna Marie wondered.

"Well, I struggled with it for a long time. Finally, I gave it to God."

"Gave it to God?" Anna Marie wrinkled her nose. "What's that supposed to mean?"

"I just let Him take control of my life. I said, 'God, I don't like what's happening. You're in charge. Help me.'"

"And it worked?"

Lexi shrugged and lifted her palms. "I'm still here, aren't I? And doing okay. I have some great friends. I like Cedar River school. Things have a way of working out, especially if you give God a chance to work in your life."

"Well, you didn't run into a Mr. Cartwright."

"No, I didn't, but I don't think Mr. Cartwright is worth hurting yourself over." Lexi thought about Egg and the steroids the teacher had offered him. "I don't think Mr. Cartwright has his students' best interests at heart. Besides, Anna Marie, you shouldn't compare yourself to others. You're special just like you are."

"That's easy for you to say, Lexi."

"That's right. It is easy for me to say because I believe it. I'll be your friend if you weigh two hundred pounds or if you weigh ninety. That's not what counts."

"It is to most people," Anna Marie pointed out.

"Well, you are going to have to put that idea out of your head, and think about what is best for you, Anna."

"Yeah, maybe you're right. My way of solving the problem sure isn't working."

"I'm curious, Anna, why are you always interested in getting recipes from people?"

"I don't know. I guess cooking and watching others eat is as good as eating it myself. Maybe even better, because that way, I can't get fat."

"So what's next?" Lexi said finally.

"They want me to start eating." She sounded frightened. "I don't want to. It's going to start all over again, Lexi, I know it is. I'm going to blow up like a balloon and people will laugh at me again, and—"

"I don't believe that, Anna Marie, and you shouldn't worry about it either. You're pretty, you have a great personality, and a lot of people like you—Jennifer, Binky, Todd, Harry. We liked you before and we like you now. And remember, Anna Marie, God loves you just as you are. He always has and He always will."

She gave a weak smile and reached out to Lexi from beneath the blanket. "Thanks, Lexi," she said, squeezing her hand.

"I hope I've been some help. Take care now, and I'll see you again soon."

As Lexi walked toward home, her mind was filled with thoughts of Anna and Egg. *If our bodies are really God's temple, we can be pretty poor caretakers.*

Chapter Nine

When Lexi arrived at school on Wednesday morning, the halls were buzzing with commotion. Jennifer ran up to her, her eyes sparkling with mischief.

"What's going on, anyway?" Lexi asked, looking around at the milling students. "Why isn't anyone going to their classes?"

"You mean you haven't heard yet?"

"Heard what?"

"Mr. Cartwright is not in his office today," Jennifer announced, as if that were highly unusual.

"So? He's probably in the gym."

"No, he's not there either."

"The weight room?" Lexi mused, not understanding what was going on. "Why does it matter where Mr. Cartwright is anyway?"

Just then Todd came up. Lexi turned to him, "Maybe you'll tell me what's happening. What's all the excitement over the fact that Mr. Cartwright isn't around this morning?"

"You got me, I just got here myself. Spill it, Golden. What's up?"

"Well," Jennifer said, relishing the task of being the bearer of such a juicy tidbit. "There's a rumor that Mr. Cartwright was arrested last night."

"Arrested?" Todd and Lexi stared at Jennifer in unbelief.

"The coach caught him trying to sell steroids to the seniors on the football team. Somebody spilled the beans about Mr. Cartwright's 'magic pills.' He'd told the students it was a surefire way into the college of their choice."

Todd hit his forehead with the heel of his hand. "I can't believe I'm hearing this."

"I'm sure it's true," Jennifer said. "Apparently, Mr. Cartwright's been talking ever since he got here about the fact that some of our guys are pretty small and could really use some building up. It wasn't until recently that anyone realized he wasn't talking about diet and exercise, but steroids."

"And he's really been arrested?" Lexi said, still unbelieving.

Jennifer nodded. "I guess the coach turned him in. That's what's going around anyway."

The warning bell rang and Jennifer headed down the hall, waving. "Gotta go. We'll talk later. See you."

Todd reached for Lexi's hand and gave it a squeeze. "You know, Lexi, I've always believed that God answers prayer, but I've never experienced it quite this—"

"—directly?" she finished for him.

He nodded. "I knew what was happening with Egg was wrong, but I didn't want to blow his cover. I didn't want him to get into trouble. So I prayed for help." Todd grinned sheepishly. "And I got it. Double strength."

It was difficult for Lexi to hold back the tears. *God does that sometimes,* she thought. *Just when you aren't sure He's listening, He answers your prayers in ways you could never have imagined.*

"I wonder where Egg is?" Todd thought aloud, "Maybe I'd better go look for him."

Lexi nodded. "He may need you right now."

He gave her hand a quick squeeze. "Talk to you later."

Lexi nodded as she watched him disappear down the hallway, then made her way to class.

———

At the noon hour, an announcement came over the loudspeaker system that the student body and faculty were to meet in the gym for last hour. Though no direct reference was made to Mr. Cartwright, everyone in the school knew what the meeting was about. At two forty-five, the students began filing into the gym, whispering among themselves. The school principal, Mr. Link, moved toward the podium with a somber expression.

"Students and faculty," he began, "I am saddened to have to call this meeting, but some events have recently transpired in our school that need to be addressed. I believe that a public forum is the best way to handle the situation. You young people are practically ready to step out into an adult world. For any of us to gloss over the incident which has occurred here this week would be foolhardy." The gym was totally silent.

"As you have no doubt heard, someone in our school has been trying to sell students anabolic steroids. Some of you may wonder what they are, while others know full well their use and purpose.

"Athletes, both male and female, wanting to acquire scholarships into colleges, are often tempted to do everything within their power to make themselves more appealing candidates."

An uncomfortable rustling and whispering went through the gym.

"Anabolic steroids, a synthetic copy of the male hormone testosterone, are drugs that promise fast muscle enlargement and increased strength. Only licensed physicians may lawfully prescribe these drugs. However, they have become readily available in body building and athletic circles. It is even more deplorable to know that these drugs are being distributed to young people who are not fully grown, because they have been known to cause stunted growth, deformities and sterility."

The faces of hundreds of students registered shock. Egg McNaughton was not excluded. His face was as pale as a sheet of paper, making his freckles stand out in contrast.

"Steroids are not a magical pill," Mr. Link raised his voice for emphasis. "Although they can make the athlete stronger, larger, and more muscular, it is not without cost to the body. In the hand of a skilled physician, steroids are an excellent remedial drug, but if used indiscriminately, they can do untold damage.

"Anabolic steroids upset the body's natural chemistry. It is suspected they may even bring on heart attacks by causing the arteries to harden and thicken. Young athletes have not been excluded in cases of heart attack and stroke brought on by these suspect drugs.

"Ironically, they can do just the opposite of what they're expected to do. As well as strengthening muscle tissue, steroids can weaken it. For young people, there are other side effects, including acne and stunted bone growth. And because steroids can make the user feel energetic, when he quits taking them, he often experiences weariness and deep depression."

Egg grew paler the longer Mr. Link spoke. He unconsciously gripped the edges of his seat until his knuckles were white.

"I just want to conclude by saying that anabolic steroids have no place in the locker room of professional athletes or college athletes, and less in that of high school athletes. Steroids do *not* solve problems, they only create them."

Although Mr. Cartwright's name was never mentioned, everyone knew that the student teacher was in deep trouble. After the meeting, Lexi waited for Egg and Todd. Egg was still pale and trembling.

"Egg-o, my man," Todd quipped, "I think we should go to the Hamburger Shack." Todd led his friend by the arm toward the door. When they found Todd's blue car in the parking lot, Egg climbed into the back seat without comment, and Lexi slid into the front. None of them spoke until they were at the Hamburger Shack, hidden in a private booth at the back of the restaurant.

After a waiter had taken their order, Egg folded his hands in front of him and leaned his forehead against his thumbs.

"I almost blew it, didn't I?" he finally spoke. "I

wanted something so badly I was willing to risk everything to get it. I never even questioned Mr. Cartwright. I thought that if he told me something would be good for me, it would be. It's like Mr. Link's reference to 'magic pills'—I wanted to believe in magic." Egg shook his head slowly. "I feel so-ooo stupid."

"You're not the only one in the whole world this has happened to, you know," Todd said to encourage his friend. "Lots of guys want to get results the fast, easy way. Everybody wants a magic pill, Egg. Some of us just have to learn the hard way that there isn't one."

"I'm just thankful that I didn't take those pills." Egg shuddered. "I kept looking at them in my drawer, thinking, 'Should I? Shouldn't I?' I guess deep down in my gut, I knew it was wrong." He looked miserable. "I even yelled at Binky because of the dumb pills. I knew I shouldn't have them, otherwise I wouldn't have been afraid she'd find them and tell our folks. Still, I couldn't give them back. I couldn't quite say no."

"But you didn't say yes, either," Lexi pointed out. "I know how hard that must have been for you. I know how much you admired Mr. Cartwright."

Egg groaned miserably. "I should have just accepted myself the way I am. Skinny, ugly . . ."

". . . kind and bright and funny. . . ." Lexi added.

"Thanks, Lexi, but nothing you can say will make me feel any better right now. No girl will look at me. Why should anyone be interested in a guy who looks like a scarecrow in a cornfield?"

Todd's fist came down hard on the table. "Now,

just a minute, Egg McNaughton. I'm getting sick and tired of your whining."

Lexi stared at Todd, amazed. She'd never seen him upset with a friend before. His unusual action even snapped Egg out of his negative slump.

"I realize that Minda is looking straight through you and she's the one you want to impress most of all," Todd said frankly, "but have you ever given any of the other girls in this school a try?"

Egg blinked, looking surprised, as if the idea had never occurred to him.

"There are a lot of nice girls in this school," Todd went on. "They aren't all like Minda—a lot of them are better. They're just as pretty and twice as nice. And they won't reject you just because you haven't got big muscles or lots of money or drive a flashy car."

"I don't know. . . ." Egg was uncertain.

"Of course you don't know! You've never tried. You've been so intent on impressing one person that you haven't even noticed the other girls around you."

"But, if Minda doesn't like me, why should—"

"Sometimes I'm not so sure Minda likes anybody, including herself," Todd said abruptly. "Give up on Minda. She's not for you. You'll have to accept that. Maybe when you do, Minda may even wake up and realize that she's missed something special in you. But she's not worth risking your health over. No girl is."

"Yeah, I guess you're right, Todd. There are a couple of pretty nice girls in my English class. . . ."

"A-hah!" Todd pointed a finger at him, grinning as only Todd could. "It's like my mom always says, 'There are lots of fish in the sea.' And there are lots of girls in this high school, Egg—nice girls who'd be impressed by who you are, not what you look like."

"Do you really think so?" Egg said, looking slightly hopeful.

"I really do. You had a close call, Egg, a very close call. I think it serves to teach us all to accept our bodies as they are."

Egg sat quietly for a long moment. When he looked up, his eyes were clearer and brighter. "I think I need to go home guys," he said. "For one thing," he said sheepishly, "I need to apologize to Binky. As much as I hate to admit it, I've been pretty rotten to her lately. Maybe I can make it up to her somehow."

Lexi put her hand on Egg's arm. "Binky just wants you back, Egg, the way you were."

"Really? Maybe I should go start up one of our old honest-to-goodness fights like we used to have."

Lexi laughed out loud. "I don't think that's the best way to handle it, but I do think that Binky would appreciate an apology."

"I need to sit down and think this through," Egg admitted. "I feel shaky, just like I had a near miss with a fast-moving car. Does that make any sense?"

"You did have a near miss, Egg. It makes a lot of sense," Todd agreed.

Egg reached out and poked Todd in the arm. "Okay, friend. Enough. No more lectures, okay?"

Todd held his hands in the air. "Scouts honor. No more lectures."

Egg glanced from Todd to Lexi and back again.

"You two make quite a pair, you know that?" He grinned. Lexi had a hunch that for the first time in many, many days, Egg was beginning to feel good about himself again.

Chapter Ten

Fortunately for those affected by Mr. Cartwright's underhanded sale of steroids, the turmoil over his arrest died down quickly. Babble about the incident would surely have gone on for many more days, except for the fact that it was time for the annual school carnival. Most students at Cedar River participated in the carnival in one way or another, by manning the booths, making food for the concession stands, face-painting for the small children attending, or selling balloons and tickets. Lexi and Anna Marie volunteered to make posters to promote the carnival around the city.

They covered the family room table with protective plastic, and began gathering materials for creating the elaborate posters. The carnival was the largest all-school event of the year.

Lexi, who had inherited some of her mother's artistic ability, sketched out the posters while Anna Marie added the color with paint and markers.

"You're doing a great job on the color, Anna

Marie!" exclaimed Lexi. "You have a real talent for this."

"Oh, Lexi, you're just trying to make me feel good. You know Ben and his friends could probably do as good a job. It's the sketching that counts."

"Anna, you're doing it *again*. You run yourself down. Can't you just believe that you are doing a good job and say thanks?"

Anna Marie leaned back on her chair and gaped at Lexi. "You should really consider majoring in psychology when you go to college. You always seem to know just the right thing to say."

"Not always," Lexi admitted. "There have been lots of times in the past few weeks that I haven't known what to say to you." *Or to Egg, for that matter*, she thought to herself.

"Speaking of psychology, how's your therapy going?"

"I hate it," Anna Marie said bluntly. "I didn't realize they'd ask me to go into my past and dig up all the things that happened to me when I was kid, and then talk about them."

"Really?" puzzled Lexi. "How does that affect your life now?"

"It's all tied together, at least that's what they tell me. The things that happened to us as young children have a lot to do with the person we are today. The therapist says that understanding the feelings I experienced as a child will help me to straighten out my life right now." Anna Marie sighed. "Sometimes I think it's just a bunch of garbage."

She jabbed some paint onto the poster she was working on. "I've felt bad about myself ever since I was a little girl, Lexi. If you'd look at our family photo album, you'd see what I mean. It's really gross. My family looks like a bunch of bowling balls, and I'm the roundest of all. My face is moon-shaped, and my arms and legs stick straight out from my clothes, because they're so fat." Anna Marie shook her head. "It's quite a sight."

She looked forlornly out the window for some time before she spoke again. Lexi waited, knowing it was good for Anna Marie to air these feelings with a friend.

"When I was in grade school my nickname was Gulp."

"Gulp?" Lexi echoed.

"That's right. The kids said I gulped my food down so fast no one ever saw it on the plate. Isn't that sick, Lexi?"

"Eating fast wouldn't have been a big deal if I'd been skinny, but I guess because I was fat they thought they had the right to tease me."

"Kids can be cruel sometimes," Lexi agreed.

"Especially when you're a fat kid. Remember when we had to be weighed and measured in grade school, and our eyes tested?"

Lexi nodded. "Yeah. I hated the eye tests. I was sure I would fail and have to get glasses."

"See, that's where we differ, Lexi. I never gave the eye tests a second thought. It wouldn't have bothered me if they told me I was blind. What bothered me most was stepping on that scale and someone else seeing how much I weighed. In third grade, I had a teacher who called out everybody's weight to the whole class as she weighed you. Can you believe it?

"She had little round glasses that slid down on the end of her nose. When she'd look up from the scale and announce my weight, it appeared she was being very cruel about it. She probably wasn't, now that I look back on it, but at the time it sure sounded like it to me. The kids covered their mouths and giggled because I always weighed at least twenty-five pounds more than any one else.

"I hated that teacher. In fact, I hated that entire school year. I guess that's why it feels so good to be thin. No one has a reason to poke fun at me. Instead, they worry about my health." Anna Marie shrugged. "That's not nearly as bad as being the laughingstock of the whole classroom, Lexi. You wouldn't understand that unless it had happened to you."

"I suppose that's why you were able to stay on such a strict diet."

Anna Marie nodded. "I know how much I want to weigh, and I'll do everything in my power to stay there. No one can make me gain weight if I don't want to. If my weight goes up, I'll just exercise until it drops again, no matter how long it takes."

"But Anna, you aren't even fat now." Lexi was feeling anxious again about her friend's problem.

"But I *feel* fat, Lexi. I think part of me died when Mr. Cartwright called me 'chunky' that day in Phy. Ed. I never want that to happen again."

"So you just quit eating entirely?"

"Not entirely. I have coffee for breakfast, water for lunch and maybe part of an apple. I take vitamins too, so I don't get sick."

"What about supper?"

"Oh, I just tell Mom I have lots of homework to

do and that I'll eat something in my room later. Usually I have some broth and diet gelatin."

"That's all you eat?" Lexi couldn't believe it.

"Oh, and lettuce. I eat lots of lettuce."

"I don't understand how you do it," Lexi said frankly.

"It isn't that hard," Anna Marie admitted, looking pleased with herself. "The thinner I am, the more powerful I feel—like I'm finally in control of something. I don't have to do what everybody else does. I don't *have* to eat. For once, I'm not trying to make anybody happy but myself. Nobody can make me eat if I don't want to."

"You've always wanted to please people, haven't you, Anna Marie?" Lexi said, remembering the term papers she'd typed for the High-Fives.

"I guess so, but my weight is something no one can control but myself."

"What's going to happen now?" Lexi asked. "Aren't you afraid you'll get sick?"

"The doctor said if I continue to faint a lot, or get any thinner, he'll put me in the hospital to make me gain weight. They call it 'refeeding.' But first he wants me to go to a therapist, to see if that helps. But I won't get fat again. I just *won't*!"

"What else are you supposed to do, besides go to the therapist?"

Anna Marie scrunched her face. "I'm supposed to gain some weight. I'm not supposed to diet anymore. I'm going to a dietitian too, so I can learn how to eat properly, and they want me to cut down on my exercising."

"Will you do that?" Lexi looked at her friend intently. The carnival posters had become unimportant.

"I don't know if I can."

"What makes it so hard?" Lexi questioned. "Is there anything at all that I can do to help make it easier?"

Anna Marie shrugged and gazed out the window. "It's nice of you to offer, Lexi, but—" She paused for a moment. "It's difficult for me to believe that anyone could really like me. I've always believed that if I were really thin, people *would* like me. Now that everyone seems to want me to gain weight again, it's really confusing."

"Anna Marie," Lexi said emphatically, "you have lots of friends. Lots of people who care for you."

"There are days when I wish I could just clamp my hands over my ears and forget those words that Mr. Cartwright said to me. I really think that was the turning point that got me going on the strict dieting. And now that I've gotten really thin, it's very hard for me to stop."

"Mr. Cartwright was a mixed up man, Anna Marie," Lexi said flatly. "He was hung up on bodies. He thought they had to be perfect. He didn't care anything about how healthy a person was, just how they looked. Because I'm a Christian, I look at things differently than others do. I believe that God gave us our bodies, that He created us and He made us like we are. There's that verse in the Bible that says we're His temples. If you believed that, Anna Marie, then you could let God control your life and your body. It's nice to know that you don't have to worry about every single thing that happens each day. You can just turn it over to a God who loves you and count on Him to help you."

Anna Marie looked at Lexi doubtfully.

"If you'd let God control your life, then you could be free to enjoy it. You wouldn't have to be constantly worrying about how much food you put in your mouth or how you look."

"Is that what makes you so happy, Lexi?" Anna Marie asked thoughtfully.

"Well, I know that a person can get very tired when they think they have to be in charge of everything. It's nice to just let go and let God take over. I'm not saying we never have to have any discipline in our lives, but it doesn't have to become a heavy burden when we allow God to lead us."

Anna Marie smiled faintly. "You know Lexi, before I got to know you, I always heard that you were 'one of a kind.' I wasn't quite sure what that meant, but I'm beginning to understand."

Lexi smiled too. "I know that not everyone thinks or believes the way I do, but that doesn't matter. I'm happy because of what I believe. You could be too. Think about it, Anna Marie."

"I appreciate the way you don't push your faith on people. It's just there—like it's part of you."

"It *is* part of me," Lexi said. "It's just like being an Emerald Tone or being Ben's big sister. Faith isn't something I can force onto someone else. It's something they have to find for themselves with God's help." Lexi was silent then, feeling she'd said enough. Showing her faith, not constantly talking about it, was the way Lexi believed people would come to understand what belief in God was all about.

She'd have to leave Anna Marie's problems to God. He'd work on them in His own time and way.

Changing the subject, Lexi announced, "I think these posters are looking good. When we finish them, we can start making our costumes for the carnival."

"Not for me. I'm not going to the carnival," Anna Marie said matter-of-factly.

"You aren't? I thought everyone in the school went," Lexi said in surprise. "I know I'm looking forward to it. It will be my first carnival in Cedar River."

"It may be fine for you," Anna Marie pointed out, "because you have Todd to go with. I don't have a date."

"You don't need a date for a carnival," Lexi explained. "We'll all be together. All the high school students wear costumes; I have an idea for mine already. It will be so much fun, Anna. You have to come!"

"No, I'll just feel out of place."

"You can't think you'll be the only girl there without a date."

"Well, no. I suppose there are lots that don't have dates, but—"

"See? You have no excuse." Lexi stood up and brushed the eraser dust from her jeans. "C'mon upstairs. I've got a whole trunk full of stuff we can use to make costumes. Todd and I are going as pirates. I promised to sew his costume for him. He's got a stuffed parrot that he's going to perch on his shoulder, and I'll sew a small tape recorder inside to play a tape that repeats 'Polly wants a cracker' over and over."

"What a great idea," Anna Marie said wistfully.

"I wish I could think of something original like that."

Lexi's eyes started to gleam. "I've got an idea! I saw it in a magazine. You'll love it."

Anna Marie held up her hand. "I didn't say I was going, Lexi."

"No? Well, maybe you will when you hear what my idea is."

Anna Marie hesitantly followed Lexi to the sewing room. "I'm sure my mom has some green fabric in here. All we need is enough to wrap around you from neck to toe."

"What is it I'm going to be?"

"A daisy! Your body will be the stem. Then we'll draw the petals on paper and cut them out. You'll wear them around your face, and your smile will be the center of the flower."

"A daisy?" Anna Marie thought about it for a moment, and then her eyes began to sparkle. "You know, that's really a clever idea."

"Of course it is," Lexi said with a giggle. "Let's get started."

"Wait a minute, Lexi. I'm not sure I want to get into this. I can hear it now. 'Look at Anna Marie! She's come as a wallflower!' "

Lexi groaned impatiently. "That's your negative side again, Anna Marie. You're going to be done with that, remember?"

"But, I just can't stand the thought of being teased, Lexi."

Lexi put her hands on her hips and glared at her. "Anna Marie, if someone laughs at you, laugh back. Of course you'll look silly—we all will. I'll be a pirate. Todd will have a talking bird on his shoulder! That's what this carnival is all about. Just plain *fun*."

Anna Marie thought about it a moment. "Well, I don't know—"

Lexi ignored her doubts and said, "Let's finish this flower, just in case."

———

During the lunch hour at school, Binky asked Anna Marie over the usual chatter at the table, "Are you going to the carnival this year?"

"Well, I haven't really decided yet," Anna Marie said shyly.

Lexi glanced at her, but didn't say anything.

"I think you should," Binky said. "It's always a lot of fun."

"Lexi did make me a costume," Anna Marie admitted. "She says everyone will be there."

Lexi looked around their table. Todd and Harry were in a deep discussion about cars. Jennifer was off talking to Matt Windsor, and Binky was leafing through her class assignment notebook. Egg seemed lost in a trance, glaring at the concrete block wall on the far side of the room. "Everybody *is* going to be there, Anna Marie. At least all our friends. Please come."

Lexi knew it would take a miracle to encourage Anna Marie to pull out of herself and trust that she wouldn't be hurt again.

When Anna Marie didn't respond further, Lexi left the lunch room. When she came back for her book bag, she discovered much to her surprise, and pleasure, that Egg was helping Anna Marie with her tray. They were talking about something, and Lexi saw that for the first time in a long time, Anna Marie had a genuine smile on her face.

Chapter Eleven

The gymnasium of Cedar River High School had been transformed. The folding wooden bleachers were gone, and the blank concrete block walls were bright with decorations. The scoreboard was covered, and even the smell of dirty socks could not be detected.

There were rows and rows of brightly colored booths—a balloon toss, a face-painting salon, even a kissing booth. Some students demonstrated string art, in another corner they cut silhouettes of customers' faces from black paper. A long line of people waited to have caricatures drawn of themselves. The concession stands sold ice cream, donuts, sno-cones and french fries, to name a few.

Mrs. Waverly, dressed as a dainty, blond-haired fairy, was busy sprinkling everyone in sight with stardust.

An elf, whose identity was unknown, wore felt shoes that curled up at the toes, and had a nose so long it bumped into the people in front of him. He kept twittering that the sky was falling.

Even Minda Hannaford had gotten into the costume mode of things. She and Jerry had come as Tweedle-Dee and Tweedle-Dum, holding hands and waddling through the aisles, their round bellies shaking as they laughed.

Tressa Williams was dressed in a striped leotard and tights, and wore a mask with a wide, toothy grin—a perfect Cheshire cat.

"Isn't this just great?" Todd asked Lexi. He looked very dashing in his pirate's costume. He wore a bright scarlet shirt, full black trousers tucked into high black boots, an eye patch and a huge fake mustache. The stuffed parrot on his shoulder was screeching, "Make the landlubbers walk the plank. Polly wants a cracker. Polly wants a cracker."

Lexi wore a bright gold shirt with billowy sleeves, and black pants. She also had an eyepatch, but it was beginning to itch. "I wonder how pirates managed," she said, peeking from beneath it. "This is the most uncomfortable thing I've ever worn."

"Just be glad you don't have a wooden leg," Todd leaned over and said cheerfully. "Hey, look over there! It's Binky and Harry."

Because they'd spent so much time together recently, Todd and Lexi had begun to tease them about being Siamese twins. For the carnival, they'd taken that quite literally. Binky had sewn together two pairs of her father's old pants, so that they shared one of the legs. She did the same with two old dress shirts. With their arms around each other, they each only needed one sleeve. It was quite a sight to behold, and because Harry was taller than Binky, they hobbled along to match each other's pace.

"I knew it would happen eventually," Todd grinned. "They really are Siamese twins."

"What a clever idea," Lexi said as the two approached them.

"Have you guys seen Chad?" Todd asked. "You can't miss him. He's ten feet tall."

Lexi laughed and pointed. There was Chad towering above the crowd on stilts.

While everyone was admiring his skill at walking on them, he stumbled and went sprawling to the floor. There were enough people around to break his fall, and everyone had a good laugh.

"Hey, you two!" It was Jennifer and Matt Windsor behind them. They were both dressed in black jeans, black leather jackets and boots, and carried black motorcycle helmets under their arms.

"Pretty dangerous looking," Todd said in mock surprise.

Matt laughed. "It was a strange feeling dressing in this outfit tonight. I actually used to wear this all the time when I was in the motorcycle gang."

"How does it feel, now?" Lexi asked, remembering the Matt she used to know—a dark, troubled boy who never smiled.

"It feels weird," Matt admitted. "I must have been trying to prove a point or something. I'd much rather wear it as a costume. Back then, it was all tied up with my old life, which I'd rather not think about anymore. We'll see you guys later. Have fun."

Todd jabbed Lexi in the ribs.

"Ouch! What was that for?"

"Look who just came in!" Todd whispered.

Lexi turned her attention to the entrance of the

gym. "It's Anna Marie!" she squealed. "And she's wearing her flower costume." The large paper petals bobbed as she walked toward them.

"Yeah, but look who's with her!"

There was Egg, making buzzing sounds around Anna Marie. He was dressed in an oversized, stuffed black and yellow T-shirt and wore black tights on his skinny legs. A huge stinger was stuck to his forehead. He very convincingly resembled a bumblebee flitting around a daisy.

"I love it," Lexi sighed. "I'm so glad you thought of a costume to compliment the daisy so well."

"Egg suggested it," Anna Marie said shyly, her face glowing.

Egg buzzed again. "I figured Anna Marie would already have a date for the carnival, but when she said she didn't, well—" Egg's grin explained the rest.

Lexi wanted to turn cartwheels with delight. Egg and Anna Marie were perfectly suited to each other. They would each have an understanding for their unique problems.

Todd tugged Lexi's arm. "I almost forgot. I signed you up for the peanut-rolling contest."

"The what?"

"It's easy. You just have to roll a peanut across the gymnasium with your nose. It was either that or egg juggling."

"I can't believe you signed me up, Todd. I'm going to look pretty ridiculous rolling a peanut in this costume."

On their way to the event, Egg and Todd stopped to buy food at a concession stand. Lexi squeezed Anna Marie's forearm. "I'm so glad you came with

Egg tonight. He's a great guy—lot's of fun. He can also be a wonderful friend."

Anna Marie's face lit up like a sunrise. "He already *is* a good friend. I think he really understands me. He knows what it's like not to be happy with your body."

"Especially when it looks like a daisy," Lexi teased.

"Or a *pirate*," Anna smiled.

A flicker of hope filled Lexi's heart. Perhaps Egg could help Anna Marie through the problems she was having. Maybe he was part of God's plan!

Todd and Egg returned with the food. "They just said over the loudspeaker that there's going to be a cake walk. Want to see if we can win ourselves a cake?"

"Of course!" Lexi said happily, smiling at her friends. "But this has been such a great evening, I don't know how it can get any better!"

In book #9, everything seems perfect in Lexi Leighton's world. Then Grandpa Leighton dies and Grandma Leighton comes to live with their family. Suddenly life is turned upside down. Grandma is ill and confused. Todd and Lexi have a disagreement that threatens to separate them forever. Will Lexi's faith survive?

Turn the page for a note from the author.

A Note From Judy

I'm glad you're reading *Cedar River Daydreams*! I hope I've given you something to think about as well as a story to entertain you. If you feel you have any of the problems that Lexi and her friends experience, I encourage you to talk with your parents, a pastor, or a trusted adult friend. There are many people who care about you!

Also, I enjoy hearing from my readers, so if you'd like to write, my address is:

Judy Baer
Bethany House Publishers
6820 Auto Club Road
Minneapolis, MN 55438

Please include an addressed, stamped envelope if you would like an answer. Thanks.